GOLD COUNTRY AMBUSH

te Ragan is heading south to see what the
ifornia gold rush is all about. Stopping
at a backcountry store for supplies,
p is interrupted. There he meets a
an and his handcuffed young female
ner, charged with theft and on her way
il. After seeing how much of a bully the
l sheriff is, Nate agrees to do the woman
vour. One thing leads to another and
te ends up involved with her husband,
e stolen jewellery, water rights and a
terious someone from his past. Will
e ever make it safely to California?

Gold Country Ambush

by

George X. Holmes

Dales Large Print Books
Long Preston, North Yorkshire,
BD23 4ND, England.

British Library Cataloguing in Publication Data.

Holmes, George X.
  Gold country ambush.

  A catalogue record of this book is
  available from the British Library

  ISBN   978-1-84262-595-8 pbk

First published in Great Britain in 2007 by Robert Hale Limited

Cover illustration © Gordon Crabb by arrangement with
Alison Eldred

Published in Large Print 2008 by arrangement with
Robert Hale Limited

Dales Large Print is an imprint of Library Magna Books Ltd.

Printed and bound in Great Britain by
T.J. (International) Ltd., Cornwall, PL28 8RW

CHAPTER 1

Coming in out of the glaring afternoon sun and into the coolness of the shade of a huge boulder next to the little creek reminded the rider of the peacefulness of a church, until the silence was broken by gunfire. His horse jumped as rock fragments peppered the animal's rump. He was being shot at!

Swinging quickly out of the saddle and dragging his Winchester with him, he slapped the horse and ducked behind the boulder. Not exactly sure where his attacker was hidden, he waited, hoping he was out of sight. Silence returned and the young man started questioning whether he hadn't imagined being fired on. Laying his dusty wide-brimmed hat to one side, he slowly edged around the gray sandstone boulder, ducking quickly back as another bullet struck the rock inches from his head. He hadn't been imagining it.

He levered a shell into the breach and peered round the other side of the rock. Nothing. Leaving his hat on the ground, he took a deep breath, jumped up and ran into the cover of the trees. As fast as the unseen gunman could work the lever of his rifle he fired at the running man. Now with a screening of trees and low-lying brush, the young man settled back to wait. Sooner or later his assailant would have to make a move.

The faint sound of moving water reminded him of his thirst. All morning and well into the afternoon, he had ridden through a landscape that seemed to change with every mile. Having left the little community of The Dalles on the Columbia River right after breakfast, he had planned on reaching Shaniko before nightfall. Riding along at a ground-eating pace, he was surprised as the countryside changed. Close to the big river, anywhere water could be pumped from a stream, farmers were busy plowing the rich soil. But very quickly, just a few miles from the wide, deep river bottom, the dry, nearly barren country took on another color; dry, treeless brown.

Then as the pale green of the sage and bile-yellow of the clumps of dried bunchgrass took over, the view turned monotonous. Nooning at the first shady spot he'd seen in hours, he had then ridden on, looking for water. His canteen was still more than half-full, but with a horse and pack-horse to water, that wouldn't last through the day. Spotting the creek, he'd smiled and dropped off the trail, only to run into trouble.

Keeping a close watch on the rocky hillside, he waited and watched. A young man just recently celebrating his twentieth birthday, he had never been shot at before. Growing up on the other side of the Columbia River he had worked with his father and elder brother in the family general store since he was old enough to pick up a fifty-pound sack of flour. He'd taken a job on a nearby cattle ranch, where he learned to work livestock. Now, with his life savings secure in a money-belt hidden under his shirt, he was off to California.

Just under six feet tall, his sun-bleached cotton shirt and denim pants were dust-covered and, he hoped, would be almost invisible in the dappled shade of the trees. Again he waited. Thinking about moving to a new spot, he stopped. A movement near a jumble of rocks near the top of the hillside opposite of where he waited caught his eye. For a time, nothing moved, and then he saw it, a slow movement close to the ground. He brought the rifle to his shoulder and aimed at the spot. There. Once again the rock seemed to move. It was a leg, a dusty, brown, pants leg. The shooter had to be lying down behind the rocks, waiting for something to shoot at.

Nate waited. When the leg didn't move he set his sights just below it, took up the slack on the trigger and fired. Knowing he hadn't hit the shooter, he quickly levered another shell and fired again, aiming at the rock the unseen man was behind. Moving a little to one side, behind an even bigger tree, he watched the hiding-place of the ambusher.

Suddenly the man came up, firing as fast as he could work the lever, spraying the trees with bullets. As the hammer struck empty, the man was up and running, dropping out of sight over the ridge. Nate, safe behind his sheltering tree, listened as the sound of a running horse faded.

Nate waited until silence once more covered the little creek bottom. Even then he used caution when he moved. Walking back into the trees, he found his horse with the reins snagged on a low tree-limb, calmly chomping at the grass at its feet. He led him back to the stream and let the animal drink a bit before tying the reins to a bush close to another small patch of grass.

Hunkering down, he ducked his head under water, took a mouthful, and set back on his heels, letting the water stream down off his face. He listened to the movement of the water and the tiny birds that flitted from one place to another, trying to relax, trying to make some sense out of the gun battle. He shook his head, then became aware of a low moaning noise. He reacted by rolling back away from the creek and lay with his Navy Colt filling his hand.

Another weak moan coming from the boulders across the stream brought him to his feet. He splashed through the shallows, pushed around the big rock and with the hammer back on the sixgun, drew down on the man lying in a crevice. Seeing the blood on the man's face, Nate holstered his Colt and knelt.

'Hey, old-timer, what the hell happened to you?' he asked. The blood, he saw, came from a gash across the man's forehead. Another low groan escaped the wounded man's lips. He hurried back to his horse, grabbed his canteen and filled it from the creek. He let a dribble wet the man's lips. Seeing a worn, shapeless hat nearby, Nate gently lifted the man's head and placed the hat under it like a pillow. He wet his neck scarf and gently bathed the man's forehead. The wound was more of a furrow, as if he'd been shot.

'Thanks, mister.' The wounded man's voice was weak, almost a whisper. 'I heard the shooting, did you get him?'

'No. Chased him over the ridge and heard him ride out. You know who he is?'

'Yeah. Harney. He was my partner. Caught me by surprise when we stopped to water the horses. Shot me in the back.'

Nate frowned. 'Looks like he almost got you in the head, too.'

'His first shot didn't knock me off my horse. His horse jumped when he shot me and I got off a shot. Hit his horse, I think. I was pulling the pack-horse and we took off. He caught up with me here when I stopped. Fell off my horse. Couldn't stay in the saddle any longer. I think his first shot did me in. My horse took off and when he came over the hill I tried to stop him. That's when he shot me. Guess he couldn't see me, though. I crawled in here when I heard you coming. Musta passed out. Next I know you're bend-ing over me.'

His voice was fading. Nate dribbled a bit more water over his lips. 'Why'd he shoot you?'

The wounded man's eyes came open and Nate could see the fear in them. 'I'm Calhoun. Obadiah Calhoun. Don't let him get me. Damn fool to trust him. Should've shot him when I had the chance.' Slowly as his voice faded into a faint whisper, his eyes closed. Nate was reaching to feel for a pulse when his eyes flashed open again.

This time the fear was gone and Nate thought there was a sparkle in his blue eyes. 'Won't do him any good. Joke's on him, the bastard. I hid the gold. He'll never find it.'

What seemed to start out as a laugh turned into a coughing fit. 'He and me, we found a good pocket of washed gold on down in the gorge. Dug it clean and was heading for Oregon City to cash out. I shoulda shot him back there. Ah, well.' His body relaxed. 'He won't find the saddle-bags. I just had to cut the ties loose and the bags fell into the hole. He rode out, you said? Then he found the pack-horse. Shooting me did no good.'

Looking straight into Nate's eyes, he nodded. 'You bury me, will ya? You go find the gold and keep riding. Don't trust nobody. Look back over the ridge a piece ... some kind of black lava-flow to the right ... a pile of rock chips the crack in the black rock ... you find it and keep riding.'

11

Nate could only watch as the light faded from the man's eyes. Obadiah Calhoun was dead.

CHAPTER 2

Four days after leaving Shaniko, Nate found himself riding through a series of rolling hills, each identical with the next and the last. He stopped at the top of one to give his horses a breather. He looked around. Straight ahead, out of sight from where he sat, he had been told to watch for a wide, shallow river and, if he hit it right, a building housing a store and saloon.

The sun was just past the midday zenith when he came to a point on the rim rock he'd been told to look for. He had done as the old man, Calhoun, had asked and buried him where he lay. He covered the body with gravel and then larger rocks to protect it from animals. He'd ridden across the creek and up on the ridge but couldn't see any one place that looked any different. From that vantage point, Nate could see what looked to be mile after mile of lava flows. Back up on the trail, he rode on into the small town of Shaniko. After telling the local sheriff what he knew, he had supper in the town's only restaurant and slept that night in a hotel bed.

'Oh, yeah,' the lawman had said. 'Old man Calhoun is pretty well-known around here. So's his partner, Amos Harney. Both of them catch all the blame when some sheep are missing or a cattle rancher loses some stock. Nobody ever saw them doing it, though. Personally, I think they simply ran a small jag of livestock on over to Oregon City and sold 'em. There's a lot of country out here and the distances make it damn hard to discover any stock missing, giving them lots of time to sell out and drink up the money.'

Nate decided not to say anything about the old man having hidden some gold. There probably wasn't anything to it and no reason to get a bunch of freeloaders out there digging everything up. Gold seemed to cause people to do odd things. Look at him, riding all the way to California even now, when the gold-rush down there was about over.

'Yeah,' he said after thinking about it a bit and changing his mind, 'the old man said he and his partner, this Harney, had found a pocket of gold and that was what had gotten

13

him shot. The joke, he said, was on Harney. Said he'd hidden the gold where it wouldn't be found. He was laughing when he died.'

After getting his directions and filling his saddle-bags with a few days' supplies, Nate rode on, leaving the story and the shooting behind him. It was, he decided, something for the local law to worry about. He was heading for California and wanted to get there before all that gold had been dug up.

Now sitting his horse on the edge of the rim rock, he looked almost straight down a couple hundred feet to a shallow river. Stretching away from the river, the flat land continued. Down below, in a bend of the river, the rider could see a patch of green and what looked like a long, narrow cabin. From what he had been told, that would be Powell's Store.

The trail, such as it was, dropped down off the rim rock and up to the porch of the cabin. Nate Ragan splashed across the shallow rocky-bottomed river, and studied the log cabin. A weathered sign was nailed to the edge of the porch roof. It said simply, STORE – BAR.

He tied his horses to the porch rail alongside half a dozen hip-shot horses and stretched the kinks out of his back. Then he stepped up on to the porch and pushed through the plank door. He stopped inside to let his eyes adjust to the dark interior. Then he took off his wide-brimmed hat and gloves, and looked casually around the room. On his right, a bar, stained by years of having liquids of questionable origins spilled on it, ran down one side of the room. A line of small tables with chairs around them was strung out opposite the bar.

Six or seven men, slouched in chairs around a couple of the tables far to the back, sat silently, staring back at the newcomer. Nate nodded to the men and walked over to the bar. The bartender, a fat man needing a shave, leaned against the wall behind the bar and watched Nate.

'Howdy. You got any cold beer?' Nate asked, the idea of something icy-cold making his mouth water.

'I got beer,' the fat man answered, not moving. 'Ain't any colder than the whiskey or anything else hereabouts. But it's wet.' Then as if as an afterthought, he said in the same toneless voice, 'Two bits.'

Nate nodded, reached into a pocket and dropped a coin on the counter. 'Sign says store.'

'Yeah,' the bartender said as he placed a

glass of foamy yellow beer in front of Nate. He picked up the coin in the same motion and pointed to the back.

Smelling the strong odor of yeast Nate tried not to breath too deeply as he took a swallow of the bitter liquid. The second sip was a little better; Nate figured his taste-buds had been shocked by the first. Glass in hand, he turned to lean back against the bar. The others were no longer paying any attention to him, he noticed.

'How far on into Farewell Bend?' he asked over his shoulder.

'The trail goes back up on the rim rock and then kinda south, about two, three hours ride, 'less'n you're in a hurry.'

Nate thanked the bartender with a nod and relaxed. It was a lot cooler in the room than outside, anyhow. He decided he would drink his beer, get a couple of cans of some-thing for supper and then ride on, spend the night in Farewell Bend. He had been told it was the largest community in this part of the state, so it should have a hotel. Sleeping in a bed with maybe a tub bath would feel good.

From what he had been told, he had another hundred miles or so of the sage-brush-covered, dry country to cross before getting back into mountains with real trees.

As he leaned against the bar, he felt his muscles relax, until he heard the sounds of the door being shoved open and of boots scraping as men's feet stepped into the dark room. Nate didn't know it but that was the last time he would have a relaxed feeling for a long time.

CHAPTER 3

When the saloon door opened, two men came in, seen only as shadows, the smaller one in front, the larger kicking the door closed behind him. The first thing Nate Ragan noticed was that the smaller person was a woman.

The young cowboy frowned as an exclamation from one of the men sitting at a table further back in the room indicated that others saw the same thing.

'Will ya look at that,' a whiskey-roughened voice from somewhere in the back said, almost with reverence. She was wearing what looked like a man's shirt, tucked into a pair of dark pants, held up by a wide leather belt. The shirt had been white, but was now dirty with trail dust. Her shoulders were proudly squared, pulling the darkened cloth tight against her breasts. In shadow, Nate couldn't see her face, but he bet it was equally proud.

Nate's frown deepened as his eyes traveled down her darkly tanned arms. She was handcuffed.

'Over there, Miz Harmon,' her companion said, taking her arm and roughly directing her toward one of the tables nearest the door. Nate looked closely at the man. From his unshaven jaws to the scruffy-looking boots, he didn't look like someone to fool with.

The man was big. Nate figured he would stand two or three inches taller and weigh thirty or forty pounds more than his own six-foot frame. Thick-muscled, wide shoulders stretched his shirt tight, almost to bursting. A shiny silver star hung from the front of the man's greasy-looking cowhide vest. On his right hip a pistol hung low in a well-oiled holster.

The woman settled herself wearily in the chair the big man motioned to, her back to the room. The badge-toting man threw himself into the second chair at the table, cuffed his sweat-stained hat to the back of his head and called out to the bartender.

The building was long and narrow, the

front part taken up by a bar that was no more than a wide, hand-hewn plank held up by a couple whiskey barrels. To the rear, half-hidden in the gloom, was a set of shelving holding canned goods. Behind the makeshift bar, as if protecting the few dingy whiskey bottles, lounged the bartender.

At the order of the lawman, the fat, scowling man behind the bar stirred. Until then, from the time the pair had come in the door, nobody in the place had moved. All were watching the woman and the big lawman. Only Nate, from where he stood leaning against the bar, had had a brief glimpse of her face.

In a brief instant as she settled in the chair, before the floppy hat she wore hid her face, he saw that it was a young face, pale skin unwrinkled but streaked where tears had cut through the dust. Now her head was bowed; he wasn't able to see much of her features. Her hair had been pulled back and hung in a long braid down her back. Dust lay thick on the braid making it look like a worn catch-rope left too long in the drying sun. The young man couldn't tell what color it would be if washed out. That didn't matter, he decided. The lawman was obviously doing his job and it wasn't any business of

19

his. This was law business and like it or not, he wasn't part of it and didn't want to be part of it.

Nate turned back to the bar, picked up his glass and drank off the rest of his beer.

Nate tried to ignore the pair, but couldn't help overhearing the lawman order whiskey from the bartender. Turning back to lean against the bar, Nate looked once again at the pair.

'What the hell you looking at?' the lawman said to Nate, his voice a sneer. 'Don't think for a minute you're going to get any of this. She's all mine. You best go back to drinking your beer and minding your own business.'

Nate knew what the bigger man saw. Nothing to be afraid of, for sure. From years of watching people and dealing with them as a trader, he knew his appearance was deceptive. Most folks, first seeing him and thinking by his young looks that he would be an easy mark in a trade, made it easy for Nate to read another's expression. He knew what the bigger and meaner-looking man was seeing. But Nate wasn't going to get involved.

'This woman is my prisoner, so don't anyone get any ideas,' the big man said to the room at large.

'That's the widow Harmon, ain't it,

Dutch?' a man at one of the tables asked. 'What'd she do to get herself handcuffed?'

'None of your damn business. This is a matter for the law and that's me,' Dutch answered, glancing at the woman with the same sneer he'd had when looking at Nate. Turning toward the bar, looking not at Nate, but at the bartender, he asked in a louder voice. 'Where in hell is my whiskey?'

Dutch took the glass of brown liquid from the bartender, tossed it back and handed back the glass. 'This time make it a full glass, damn you,' he snarled.

As he sipped the second glass of whiskey, he looked at the girl. 'Yeah,' he said looking at the girl but speaking to everyone in the room, 'this here's the widow of that shyster Jess Harmon, all right. Her husband was a crooked card-player and she's a thief,' he said. Nate was learning that everything the big man said was with a sneer, it seemed to be his normal voice.

'Naw,' the man who had asked the question said. 'I worked for her father a long time, back before he died. I knew her before she married that Harmon. She weren't no thief.'

'Hell she ain't. When Banker Runkle and his wife put her up at their house, the very next day jewelry belonging to Mrs Runkle turned up missing. The sheriff deputized me to go out to bring her back to stand 'fore the judge. Yeah, she's a thief all right.'

Nate watched the woman's head sink lower against her chest as her captor told everyone of her crime. 'Hey, bartender, gimme another whiskey,' the deputy said. Briefly, the woman's head came up and she looked directly into Nate's eyes, then away.

After taking another glass of whiskey to the table and returning to the bar, Nate remembered that no one had offered the woman anything to drink.

'Barkeep,' Nate said, 'get me a glass of water, will you?'

The bartender looked quickly at Dutch, then at the woman and then back at the younger man. Studying Nate for a moment, the bartender dipped a glass of water from a bucket behind the bar and placed it in front of him before walking to the other end of the bar.

Nate picked the glass up in his left hand and carried it over to the woman.

'Here, Mrs Harmon,' he said quietly.

'Hey, get away from her,' the deputy said, reaching for the water. 'She's my prisoner and I'll be the one to take care of her needs.'

Looking directly at the deputy, Nate said, his voice quiet but clear, 'She needs a drink.'

Raising her handcuffed wrists, the prisoner took the glass in both hands and drank deeply.

The deputy, tearing his eyes from Nate, lunged to knock the glass from her mouth. Before he could finish the move, though, the gun barrel Nate had jammed into his stomach stopped him.

'That's enough,' Nate said warningly, thumb cocking back the hammer of his .44 Colt. The pistol had once belonged to his father and the cedar grips were worn smooth. Nate's face didn't waver as he thought about the bad fix if he had to pull the trigger. This was the first time he'd ever pulled a gun on a man and he wasn't sure he could shoot if he had to.

The deputy froze, half-leaning over the table. Slowly, without taking his eyes off Nate's, he settled back in his chair.

'Barkeep, bring the lady another glass of water, please,' Nate's voice remained unhurried.

'Thank you,' the woman said in a small voice, holding the second empty glass out to the young man. Taking it again in his left hand, Nate stepped back to the bar, holstering his pistol, never taking his eyes off the seated man.

With a shake of his head, and a yell at the bartender for more whiskey, the deputy relaxed in his chair, glaring at Nate.

Feeling the danger was over, Nate let his eyes drift over to the woman. For the first time he saw that she was only a girl, not much older than he. Her clear blue eyes looked at him and then drifted down to the handcuffs.

Dirt and dust had darkened her skin, but under it all he could tell she was tanned from working outdoors. Her face was pleasantly rounded, her chin hinting at an inner strength. Full lips, cleaned by the water, were a healthy pink color. He wished he had seen her smile. I'll bet she has a beautiful smile, Nate thought.

'That's taking a hell of a risk, cowboy,' the deputy said. 'Coming in between the law and his prisoner like that could get you in trouble.'

Nate didn't respond, but simply watched the man.

The girl's head stayed bowed, as if she was staring at the handcuffs. Blue eyes, Nate thought. The deepest blue eyes he had ever seen.

He didn't know much about women. There had been a few that came into the store, but he was always too busy to pay much attention. Or else afraid that, getting too close to one, he might end up with a family he didn't want. At least not until he had seen a bit more of the world.

Now here he was, in a scrubby little saloon perched next to a shallow tread of a river in the middle of a desert, taking a glass of water to a girl with beautiful blue eyes. Shaking his head, he told himself he couldn't let that bother him. He was on his way to California.

Still thinking about how Mrs Harmon's blue eyes seemed to look deep into his soul, Nate walked to the back of the room and looked through the collection of tin cans until he found one with a picture of peach-slices, all yellow and wet looking, on the label.

He couldn't help but think of her eyes, though. Eyes so deep it was almost like looking into the big pool in the river where he fished as a kid. Taking the can of peaches back to his place at the bar, he heard the deputy laugh.

'Naw, we ain't staying for no meal here. I'm taking her into town and she's going straight to jail.'

'That's too bad, Dutch,' one of the older men sitting toward the back of the saloon said. 'You'll take her into jail and they'll send her over to some prison and nobody'll get anything from her. You ought to be letting us have some fun with her before you go riding her into town.'

Nate placed the peach can on the bar and walked back to the speaker's table. The man's eyes shifted away as he saw the look in Nate's eyes. Sweat broke out when he looked down to see that Nate had already taken the strap over the hammer of the pistol.

'What were you asking about?' Nate asked.

He watched as the man blanched and carefully brought his right hand up to wipe the moisture from his face. Looking quickly at the men sitting next to him, he watched them slowly push their chairs away from the table, away from him.

'Nothing. I wasn't asking nothing, just talking my fool head off, that's all.'

Nate stared at the man for a moment before relaxing, and with a slow look around at the others sitting at the table, turned and walked back to the bar. Once again he motioned to the bartender with his empty glass.

Nate took a bone-handled pocket-knife from a pants pocket and, after dropping a few coins on the bar, cut open the can. Tilting the can back, he was drinking the thick, sweet juice, when he heard the deputy's voice.

'Well, Miz Harmon, I guess it's about time we got on our way.' Without looking, Nate knew the sneering smile was back on the burly deputy's face.

The bartender, corking the whiskey bottle and picking up the change the lawman had dropped on the table, looked quickly at the handcuffed prisoner.

'It's still early enough to get to Farewell Bend before dark, but you'll have to step it up a little.'

'Naw.' Nate could hear the sneer in his voice. 'We'll probably have to camp somewhere along the way and go on in tomorrow morning. Don't want to tire my horse, you see.' Hearing a sharp gasp from the woman and a chuckle from the back of the room, Nate didn't bother to turn. Using his pocket-knife, he speared one slice of peach and then another.

'Coming, little lady?' The big man once again took her arm and roughly pushed her toward the door. 'Time to get travelin'.'

Nate placed the empty can on the bar,

27

reached up to settle his hat firmly in place, glanced back at the seated men, nodded to the bartender and followed the pair outside.

The girl was already seated in the saddle, when Nate pushed through the door and stepped out on to the porch, her manacled hands holding the saddle horn, her horse's reins in Dutch's free hand. The deputy halted as he was about to swing up into his saddle and turned to face Nate.

'Where in hell do you think you're going?'

'Why, I'm headed to Farewell Bend myself, and it's about time for me to be traveling, too.'

'Damn you, don't mess with me or you'll get more than you wanted,' Dutch said, dropping the reins and letting his hand settle on his holstered pistol.

'I don't plan on it,' Nate said quietly. 'Just going to ride along behind so as not to lose my way.' Looking past the deputy's stormy face, Nate saw a quick smile on the woman's face before she once again let her chin drop against her chest.

The deputy turned quickly, swung into the saddle and hustled his prisoner away.

CHAPTER 4

Nate crossed the river and followed the two riders, with the handcuffed woman in front and the deputy sheriff close behind, as they made their way single-file up the series of switchbacks to the top of the rim rock. Without a word being spoken, the three stopped to let their horses blow. Looking back, Nate could see Powell's Store far below and the river winding in a snakelike track through the wide valley floor. Far off to the east, a bluish haze indicated tree-covered mountains.

Cursing, the deputy jerked his horse around, pulled the girl's horse after him, and started off again. The strange parade rode at a good clip for a mile or so, before the leader slowed his horse to a walk. They held that pace for the next hour.

Keeping one eye on the deputy, Nate took time to look at the country they were riding through. It was obvious they were still in the high desert. Sagebrush and clumps of brown bunchgrass covered nearly every foot of sandy soil. One major difference was the size of the junipers. Where before they were mostly just low-lying bushes, now they grew in taller clumps, almost trees, some twenty-feet tall or more. Instead of being able to see in any direction for miles, now a rider could only see short distances. Random outcroppings of rough lava rose in places, sometimes towering over the juniper trees, other times jutting up higher than a man on horseback. Far ahead, Nate could see what appeared to be a tall, round-topped hill. The trail they were following seemed to be heading in that direction.

No words had been spoken since leaving the top of the rim rock. The deputy made no further mention about stopping for the night.

Picking up the pace once again, the three riders soon topped a low hill, Nate spotted what must have been the town of Farewell Bend. A river, much wider than the one by the saloon, wound its way alongside the main cluster of buildings. The round-topped hill was a mile or so to the east.

Coming into town from the north, Nate followed behind the other two and looked down the wide dirt street. A number of side streets branched off at irregular intervals, each little more than alleys and usually going only as far as the back of the buildings they separated. Signs hanging out over plank sidewalks told where the hotel was, and the jail, a barber shop, general store and bank. Other buildings lined up, making the main unpaved street some six blocks long on one side and four on the other. A steepled building at one end identified the town's church.

Between the main part of town and the river, running at right angles to the main business section, a row of houses lined a wide street. Picket-fences fronted a few of them, others simply had a hitching-post along the porch for visitors to tie their horses up.

The big deputy pulled his horse up in front of a small square rock building. The sign over the door said SHERIFF. Nate swung down and, before the deputy could stop him, took the woman's arm and helped her down from her horse.

'Damn you,' the deputy said, dropping his hand to his gun, 'I warned you about interfering with my prisoner.'

Before he could pull his gun, a loud voice yelled: 'Voles, damn your eyes. Why did you handcuff that woman?'

Nate turned to see who was talking and found himself face to face with a stockily built man, wearing a silver star on his vest, which had the word sheriff stamped on it. Once he had been a big, strong man, Nate figured, but now age had bent some of the bigness out of him. Steel-gray hair tufted over his ears and from his squint Nate thought he probably had trouble seeing up close.

'Well, you gonna stand there all day? Bring her in and for God's sake, get those cuffs off her.' As he turned back into the open door the older man continued talking to his deputy. 'You'd think she was a real bad criminal. Or maybe you were just a little afraid she'd get away from you.'

As the deputy unlocked the handcuffs, he indicated Nate with a jut of his chin. 'This damn fool kept getting in my way. I think you ought to arrest him for bothering a deputy while doing his sworn duty.'

'Deputy! Hell, you ain't no deputy. I just asked you to go ask Mrs Harmon to come in because that damn fool of a banker wouldn't let up on me until I did. Now, get that badge off and run along and tell your boss that you've been a good boy and done what he wanted.'

Voles scowled but took off the badge and tossed it to the sheriff. He turned abruptly, but stopped when he saw Nate watching.

'Didn't do you any good, did it, cowboy?'

'Oh, I don't know. It certainly kept you from her.' The bigger man's scowl darkened and, jerking the reins of his horse, he climbed into the saddle and kicked the animal into motion.

The sheriff turned to the woman and held a chair for her to sit in. 'I'm sorry, Mrs Harmon. I shouldn't have sent that idiot. But Runkle was bothering me something fierce and my leg was hurting so I couldn't ride. I hope he didn't cause you any trouble.'

Looking at Nate, she shook her head. 'No, thanks to this man.'

The sheriff looked Nate over from head to boot-top. 'What's your play, stranger?'

'Nothing. Just following along. I was going the same place they were, and I didn't want to get lost, so I just followed along.' Nate leaned against the open door-jamb and watched as the sheriff settled himself in the chair behind a desk.

The lawman sat with the chair sideways to his desk, his right leg straight, the knee only slightly bent. For a long minute he studied the younger man before turning to the woman.

'I'm sorry, Mrs Harmon, I truly am, but charges have been made that you stole some jewelry. I will have to keep you in custody until the circuit judge gets here to hear the case.'

Looking back at Nate, he said, 'Dutch Voles has a reputation for getting grabby around women, but I never thought he would act up while wearing the badge. Guess I should have known better.'

He slapped his right leg gently and went on: 'I took a spill a week or so ago and messed up my knee. It's getting better, but it hurts like the devil to sit a saddle, or I'd have gone myself.'

He stuck out a plate-sized hand to Nate and introduced himself. 'I'm Sheriff Roy Brickey and I want to thank you for escorting Mrs Harmon into town.' He turned back to the woman and shook his head.

'I've been sheriff here since the town was formed a few years back. This is the first time I've had a woman in custody.'

'Are you going to keep her back there?' Nate asked, pointing to the single cell that took up the back half of the cabin.

'No, I guess I'll take her over to Ida. She can get a bath and some dinner. No reason I can see to hold her in the cell for the next week or two 'til the judge gets here.'

'Who is Ida?' Nate asked.

'My wife. She's a good woman. You seem

34

to be taking a great interest in this woman, cowboy. Why?'

'Just wanted to see that she's treated fairly, Sheriff.'

'Did Dutch mistreat her?'

'No,' Nate said with a shake of his head. 'Not really. But then he knew I was watching, didn't he? I think I'll go get something to eat myself. Be seeing you, Sheriff. Ma'am,' he added, smiling as he tipped his hat toward the seated woman. He turned, gathered up his reins and swung into the saddle.

CHAPTER 5

Sarah Harmon didn't know what was going on. Ever since the morning she'd found her husband's body her mind had been in a sort of daze. Nothing made sense. He hadn't been all she had expected in a husband, but she wasn't sure, really, what to expect. Her mother had died while she was very young and being raised by a big, gruff father who was busy building a ranch in the high desert country did not give her a very clear picture of what married life was like.

Aaron Noble had been a good father, or at least as good as he knew how to be. But teaching his daughter all the things a daughter needed to know was far beyond his capabilities and he knew it. First, while living in the Willamette Valley, he had hired a woman to cook for them and care for the house. Part of the house, he figured, included his eight-year-old daughter. The cook was a big woman named Maggie. Sarah remembered that she always smelled like fresh bread baking in the oven.

That situation was just right, her father thought, until he decided to sell out and travel over the mountain to build his ranch. He'd heard that land, lots of land suitable for raising cattle and sheep, was there for the taking. Working his small acreage in the Willamette Valley was profitable, but the chance of ranching 1,000 acres was too good to pass up.

Leaving Sarah with Maggie, Aaron Noble set out and for the next three years, worked day and night to clear the land he had marked out and build a house to bring his daughter home to.

When it came time to join her father, the only bad thing was leaving her friend, the cook. She was with her father and that was

36

all that counted.

In the years to come, her father hired a succession of women to help raise his daughter. Each taught her what they could but none stayed very long. Usually, although Sarah didn't realize it, they left as soon as they discovered that the ranch owner had no desire to marry a second time. By the time she was seventeen, she had learned how to do all the things a proper girl did, but really knew little about life.

Jess Harmon was not the first full-time hand her father hired, but he was the first to be given the job of foreman. A young man, he was only five or six years older than Sarah when he came riding in, looking for work. Tall and slender, he sat a horse as though it was part of him. Black curly hair, always looking as though it needed cutting, Jess was almost too good-looking for his own good. But, as her father soon discovered, he was a hard worker.

Aaron Noble valued a hard worker. In clearing juniper and sagebrush off a large portion of the range he had claimed, he himself had worked seven days a week, from daylight to dark. Only when Sarah would stomp her foot and demand he stay home on Sunday would he do so, and then usually only for the afternoon. The rest of the time he would be found hard at it, either working on one of the rock-diversion dams he was building in the Crooked River or hand-digging one of the irrigation ditches that moved the water onto his pastures.

It was on one of the rare Sundays when her father had promised to be back at the ranch house for an early meal that her world started to fall apart. When the sun had passed the zenith with no sign of her father, she decided to ride out and give him a piece of her mind.

A very pretty girl, she was a very innocent seventeen years old when she saddled her favorite pony and headed out. Life at the ranch ran fairly smooth. She had her father. The life of work had taken a lot out of her father, and until she found him slumped over a shovel in one of the ditches, his daughter had never noticed how old he looked. For a long time she sat her horse and looked down at the only man she had ever loved.

Weeks went by, after she had buried her father, before she took any interest in life. Jess had tried a couple of times to bring a problem to her, hoping it would help bring a smile back to her face. Actually, he and the rest of the crew handled all problems as they came up, but they had decided it was one way to get the girl past her mourning. Only it didn't seem to work.

When her father had built the house, he had built a wide porch all along one side. It had been a favorite place for him to sit in the evening and think about the work that would be done the next day. One afternoon, while Jess sat in a chair on the porch talking to Sarah about the need to build a small herd to take to market, he stopped talking and simply looked at her.

Just like many other cowboys riding through, Jess had been taken by the freshness of the girl from the first day he rode up. Now, after a couple years of working on the ranch and watching her grow into womanhood, he knew he was in love with her. It took a few minutes for her to notice his silence.

'Why, Jess, what's the matter?'

'You haven't heard a word I said, Sarah. It worries me. You have to get over your father's death and start living again.'

'I know. I haven't been much help; you and the boys have been so good to me. But I just can't seem to get over it. I'm sorry, I'll try to pay more attention to you. Now, what were we talking about?'

'I asked you to marry me,' he said softly.

Seeing a frown start to ruffle her forehead, he quickly went on: 'Sarah, I don't mean any disrespect, but, well, you're all alone and I could take care of you. I would be good to you and, well...' Not seeing any change in her expression, his words faded away.

Slowly, getting to his feet, he shook his head. He placed his hat squarely on his head and stepped off the porch. 'I'm sorry. I'll talk to you tomorrow about making up a herd to run up to Shaniko. Good night.'

'Jess,' she said, her voice soft in the early evening air. 'Let me think about it. Your proposal, I mean. It just came so unexpectedly. Please, just let me think about it.'

A smile as big as the sliver of moon that had risen over the eastern rim rock spread across the cowboy's face.

'Sure. You do that. Give it a lot of thought. I ... well ... I guess I'll say good night.' He wanted to holler at the moon, and jump in the air, but held himself in all the way back to the bunkhouse. Yessir, he said to himself, it is time to settle down and become a respectable rancher, not just go on as the ramrod of other people's ranches. Yessir, it was certainly time.

They were married two weeks later in Shaniko. Sarah had helped trail the sixty-five head of yearlings up to the market town and, after the ceremony, rode back to the ranch with the crew and her new husband.

Life continued much as it had before her marriage. She wasn't sure what happened but just before their first anniversary, she knew it had been a mistake.

For the next three years or so she took care of the house and kept the ranch books while Jess worked the stock. Only in the privacy of their house was there no noticeable improvement. They were almost like strangers.

Sarah wasn't sure when she discovered that Jess had started riding into the new town of Farewell Bend. Wagon trains taking what was supposed to be a short cut had named the site on a bend of the Deschutes River. One or two of the travelers decided not to continue on, and built a store to sell goods to those who did. Soon a saloon and blacksmith shop joined the store and the town was born. Jess, she found out, was spending first one night a week then more at the saloon.

She tried to talk to him about it, but he wouldn't discuss it.

Hank had been with her father since right after Noble had first staked out his land. Hank, just like others, looked on Sarah almost as his own daughter. He didn't want to hurt her, but he didn't want Jess to hurt her either. And his first loyalty was to the ranch and Sarah was the ranch. Hank had not meant to tell her that her husband was not out with the herd as he had said he would be. And once it was said, the man didn't know how to not tell her about the gambling and drinking.

It went downhill from that time on. Life at the ranch was not the same. Until, just as when she had found her father's body, she found her husband's.

CHAPTER 6

It was Jess's horse that she saw first. The animal was standing head down, reins caught in a broken juniper limb when she rode up the trail from the ranch onto the top of the rim rock. Feeling an emptiness in the pit of her stomach, she kneed her pony over to the horse. On finding no sign of the rider, Sarah tied her horse to a branch of the same tree and began to search on foot.

Rattlesnakes were not unheard of in the rocky desert. One could have frightened the horse, throwing Jess and then bolting, only to be caught by the juniper branch so close to the edge of the rim rock. Slowly she tried to backtrack the horse.

It was a strange trail. From what she could make out, the horse had walked up to about the spot she had found it. Walked, the trail had not been left by a panicked, snake-scared horse. Of course, she was not a tracker, she said to herself. But even she could see the prints left by the horse. Only alongside, the dirt looked unnatural, as though it had been brushed.

She walked back to the tied horses, then went past them, closer to the edge of the rim rock. Far below she could see a bend of the Crooked River. Looking straight over, she saw a bit of color down the steep, rocky embankment. Far below, she watched the sun-bleached red spot for a long moment, knowing it was the same color as one of the shirts on which she had sewn a button for her husband only a few days before.

Nate climbed tiredly back into the saddle, and pulling the pack-horse's lead rope, rode down the dirt street. He rode slowly, looking first to one side then the other, reading the signs over doors and paying particular attention to the few people going about their business. Most of the men, he noticed, wore either gray canvas pants or, like himself, heavier denim pants. Only one or two wore coats or even vests in the early evening sunshine.

Looking down one of the few side streets, he could see past the building that fronted on to the main street before fading away into the sagebrush.

At the far end of the main thoroughfare, a corral large enough to pen up a couple dozen head had been built directly in line with the street. Traffic was forced to turn either right or left. A small plank shack had been built alongside the corral and Nate noticed as he got close that a man was sitting in chair, leaning back against the wall of the shack watching his approach. Nate pulled up in front of the man and sat his horse.

'This a good place to leave my horse for the night?' he asked after a while. The man, Nate thought, was probably the oldest person he had ever seen. The top half of his sun-browned face was lined so deeply, it would be impossible to shave it clean. The bottom half was covered in a beard that had probably been black or dark brown at one time, but now was a dingy light gray, streaked with the original color. Or, the rider thought as the old-timer turned his head to spit a long stream of tobacco juice, it had been dyed the color of chewing-tobacco.

Wiping a gnarled hand across his thin lips, the old man pointed to the railed corral. 'That's what it's there for. And I'm here to collect the two bits it'll cost. Half a dollar if you want to feed 'em some grain.' His voice, like the rest of him, was dry and almost featureless. 'If you're a mind to, pull your hull off'n that horse and turn him into the corral. You can hang your saddle in the shed, here, but there ain't much room. You'll probably want to leave your pack down to the trappers' cabin.' He pointed the way as he talked, the old man's chair staying tilted on its two back legs.

Nate smiled and stripped the rigging off his horses. The corral gate was not of a kind the rider had ever seen before, the opening just wide enough for a horse to pass through, about six feet wide. There were two rails, the bottom rail slid back into the stationary fence rails and the top rail, only a couple feet longer than the opening, had to be lifted off to let his animals pass through.

He hung his saddle in the shed and forked some hay into the corral before setting on the narrow porch alongside the old man.

Neither spoke for a long moment.

'You make a good living, sitting there making your customers do the work?' Nate asked in a quiet, conversational tone.

'I got the corral, hay and pitchfork,' came the quick answer. 'You got the hungry horses. Ya want ya can drag your saddle back on that animal and ride out. Lots of good grazin' out there amongst the sagebrush, I guess.'

'Not that I could see,' Nate said. He smiled and dug in his pants for some coins. He placed them in the old man's gnarled hand.

'You have time to point me toward the best place to get a hot meal, a cold beer and a soft bed for the night?'

'Shoot, I thought you was a real cowboy,' the hostler said with disgust in his voice, 'but wanting a soft bed clears up that question. Wal, I reckon the best would be the Miners' saloon. Hotel's across the street.'

Nate took his hat off and ran a hand through his long black hair. He chuckled.

'Harrrump,' the old guy snorted, 'My name's Tex,' he said, sticking a scrawny hand out to shake.

Nate introduced himself before starting to walk away, only to be stopped by Tex's dry voice. 'I seen ya ride in with that Voles fella. Was I you I'd just eat, drink, sleep and tomorra, ride on out of town.' Tex brought his chair to rest on all four legs and got up slowly, stiffly. Stretching, he turned to look down at Nate and flipped his thumb toward the open door of the hay-shed. 'Ya plan on leaving early, don't make a lot of noise. I sleep in there and need my beauty sleep, don't ya know.'

'I'll be as quiet as a church mouse. Now, head me in the direction of that cabin you spoke of and I'll store my packs.'

The log cabin, the old man said, had been built by some trappers years before the first wagon train came by. A storage place first for furs, it was used now by anyone wanting to keep his gear dry. Not that it ever rained much in this high desert country, Tex said, but he could keep his packs out of the reach of mice and other critters.

On finding the trappers' cabin, Nate hung his packs from a rafter. Old though it looked, the cabin was snug, little of the moss and mud chinking between the logs was missing. Carefully the young man shut the plank door after himself, took his bedroll, and turned back toward the street and dinner.

The Miners' saloon was like many others he'd been in: long and narrow with a bar running down one side. Tables were scattered around, taking up the rest of the room. Far to the back of the place, Nate could see a couple of felt-topped card-tables, one with a visor-wearing dealer patiently laying out a game of solitaire.

Men looked up as he walked though the double doors, but after inspecting him closely, went back to their drinks, friends or simply a spot on the wall, looking far away. Nobody paid the newcomer any further attention except for the aproned bartender. Nate asked about a glass of beer and food.

'Steak and fried potatoes,' the bartender said. 'Half a dollar.'

'Worth it if I don't have to do the cooking.'

He took a table and settled back in his chair, feeling the tension of the day melt away. Relaxed, he was just finishing the last of the fried potatoes when two men entered the saloon. Leaning back and wiping his mouth with the back of his hand, he looked up at the pair. The most noticeable was the smaller of the two. Nate figured him to be about six inches shorter than his companion, but heavy, weighing a good 200 pounds. Looking at the other man, Nate saw it was his friend, Dutch Voles.

Unlike Dutch, who was still wearing the

same dusty canvas pants and dingy vest he'd worn during the day's ride, the shorter man wore a flat-topped black-felt hat, obviously brushed clean. The hat sat squarely on his square block of a head. He stood with his back to the bar, both thumbs stuck in the small pockets of his woollen vest, which was buttoned tightly over a protruding stomach. Middle-aged, the man had the stomach of the successful saloonkeeper or banker. A man more used to a desk than the back of a horse. He was the only man in the place wearing a woollen suit. Nate thought he could see the bulge of a holstered pistol at the man's hip, under the suit-coat.

Dutch threw back the whiskey the bartender had set in front of him and turned to look over the room. Seeing Nate, he frowned and bent over to whisper in the shorter man's ear. The suited man turned to glare at Nate, then, picked up the glass left by the bartender and walked over to Nate's table.

'Howdy,' the man said. He dragged over a chair and sat down across from Nate. 'I'm John Runkle. Mind if I join you?'

Nate didn't answer. Runkle took his hat off and placed it flat on the table. Nate saw he was a little older than he had at first thought. His gray hair had been cut close to his skull and wrinkles radiated from the corners of his watery blue eyes. The eyes were small and hard-looking. Nate had the feeling that if the man smiled, the smile rarely reached his eyes.

'Dutch told me you helped bring in that thieving Harmon girl,' Runkle said, watching closely for a reaction.

Glancing over to where the burly former deputy stood, leaning against the bar, Nate didn't let any expression show on his face. A trained horse-trader, Nate felt the man across the table was looking for something and decided he didn't want to give him a thing.

'Nope, just happened to be coming this way same time they were.'

'Well, just so it is clear. I own the bank and other businesses here. And it was jewelry that belonged to my wife the girl stole. I think Dutch is right. From what he told me, you showed too much interest in her. That could get you in trouble.' The seated man didn't smile as he spoke, and his eyes seemed to get smaller, taking on a squinty stare.

Not overly intimidated, Nate for the first time smiled. 'She is a looker, all right. Hard to believe she would steal anything.'

'No question about it,' the banker said, leaning back a little in his chair. 'My wife, being a good woman, tried to help her when she needed a woman's shoulder to cry on. To show her gratitude, the little thief took the jewelry my wife's mother left her. Pretty? Yes, but a thief none the less.'

Holding up his empty glass, Runkle motioned to the bartender for another drink. Voles brought the whiskey over to the banker and at a nod from him, pulled out the chair on Nate's left and sat down.

Voles smirked as Nate, swinging his chair around so he was facing both men, said, 'Make yourself at home, gentlemen.'

'Young man,' Runkle said, showing anger, 'this is my home. You are a visitor, a visitor showing too much interest in my affairs. Drink your drink and let your supper settle. Get a good night's sleep if you've a mind to, but take some advice. Be out of town by sun-up tomorrow. There's a big world out there, go see it.'

'Or what?' Nate nodded toward Voles. 'You'll have your friendly deputy arrest me?' The big man smiled.

'Old Dutch here works for me,' the banker said. 'I only loaned him to the sheriff to bring the girl in. If I tell him to make sure you are leaving town, he will. Dutch knows quite a lot about guns and fighting, so I'd take my advice were I you.'

'Old Dutch certainly knows how it feels to have the barrel of my pistol stuck in his fat gut,' Nate said and noticed how quickly the smile that hadn't reached Runkle's eyes faded away. 'But I am just traveling through. I'll probably ride on tomorrow.'

'Boy,' Dutch's gravely voice was low and sounded as though it came from an empty barrel, 'boy, it won't be the barrel of my gun you'll be feeling I find you here tomorrow.' The voice held all the poisonous venom of a stepped-on rattlesnake.

'Well, there you are,' Runkle said, pushing back his chair and getting to his feet. 'Couldn't be plainer than that.'

Looking down at Nate, the banker's eyes again didn't show the smile that hovered around his thin-lipped smile. 'Get your ass out of my town.'

CHAPTER 7

It was easy for Amos Harney to get Ned Clarke, Shaniko's sometime sheriff and all-the-time town drunk, to talking. All it took was catching him in his favorite saloon and buying him a couple whiskeys.

'Naw, I wasn't with old Obadiah on that trip south to look for gold,' he told the lawman. 'Hell, Ned, everybody knows that story of a lost gold-mine is pure bunk.'

'Well, it seems likely. But this young fella certainly told a good story. Said he'd found Calhoun hidden in some rocks up along a little creek. Had to be one that flows into the John Day River. Not anything for me to go be interested in, so I didn't pay much attention.' He threw back his whiskey and smiled as Harney motioned for a refill.

'Did this young guy get to talk with Obadiah? You know, any last words?'

'Not really. Something about you and claimed you two had fallen out over some gold nuggets you'd found. The stranger didn't say much more'n that.'

'I wonder, maybe I should look this jasper up. After all, old Obie was a friend of mine. Did he say where he was heading?'

'Well, he did ask about the trail south. I told him about Powell's Store and how to get to Farewell Bend.'

The story he was told at the store and the bar along the river had led him here, Farewell Bend. Any information about strangers could most be easily found in a saloon and as this was the only one in town, Harney thought if he stayed quiet, sooner or later he'd find his man. He didn't have a name, but from the description he'd been given, the man sitting at one of the tables having dinner could be him. Trying to think of a way to get next to the young man, he watched as the two other men went over to his table and sat down. Maybe there was something there for him. He sauntered over and took a chair at a nearby table.

'Get your ass out of my town,' he heard the short fat man say before the two men walked away, laughing. Harney waited only to see the young man stand, then, hitching his gunbelt into place, follow the two out the door.

This could be bad, Harney thought. If he read the warning in the fat man's voice right, this young man might be in trouble, and until he had a chance to talk Harney couldn't allow anything to happen to him. He'd have to stay close, he decided.

Early the next morning, after a breakfast of steak and eggs at the Miners' saloon, Nate once again stopped by the trappers' shack. Shouldering his saddle-bags and other gear, he hiked on up to the corral for his horses. Tex was just finishing cinching down the saddle on Nate's horse when the cowboy arrived.

'Thought ya might want him this morning,' the gruff voiced man said as he finished tightening the cinch and dropping the stirrup. 'Saw ya leave the Miners' saloon and thought I'd do ya a final favor before ya ride on out.'

'Thanks,' Nate said. He dropped his packs and hunkered down against the wall of the hay-shack. 'Your little community doesn't go out of its way to make a man welcome, does it?'

'Naw. We got no time for anybody old man Runkle doesn't like,' Tex explained. He settled in his wooden chair and leaned back against the shack next to Nate. 'Owns most everything. Even owns the ditch that irrigates 'most all the pasture land around here. Without that water ain't much a man can do in this part of the world.'

'Thought I saw a river down there, at the edge of town,' Nate commented, looking up the dirt street. People had started their morning business, coming into town in wagons to shop at the general store, or simply stopping to visit with friends on the street.

Nate watched as Dutch came out of the

door of the bank and went across to disappear into the hotel.

'Wal,' Tex went on, giving no indication that he had seen Dutch cross the street, 'It would work pretty good, but somehow anyone digging a ditch seems to run into trouble. First your ditches are going to get dynamited. Or if ya had to build a diversion dam to raise the water above the riverbank, it gets destroyed, do ya see?'

'And nobody'd ever see how it happened?'

'That's the way it is,' the old man said and watched as Dutch came out of the hotel and stopped on the plank sidewalk, looking toward the public corral.

'Wonder who he's looking fer?' Tex said, glancing at Nate.

'What about Mrs Harmon?' Nate asked, watching as Dutch left the sidewalk and started down the street.

'Wal, her daddy went out and marked out a couple sections over near the edge of the big forest, north-east of here.' The old man was now watching Dutch's approach as closely as Nate was. 'He burned and pulled junipers from a big piece of land, mostly alongside a little river called the Crooked River. Flows out of that gorge and then winds all over the place, going ten miles just

56

to get three closer to where it's going. Got his water from that river. Done real good, don't ya know. The widow, Sarah, was his only child,' he said as Dutch walked up, then stopped a few feet away from the men seated in the early-morning sun.

'Hey, you son of a bitch,' the rough-voiced man said.

Nate slowly looked up at the big man. Dutch was about ten feet or so away and stood legs apart, hands on his hips.

'You were told to get. Now you got one chance to get your horse and ride.'

Nate watched the bigger man for a moment, then, standing, let a smile cross his face. 'Yeah. Well, guess that's decent of you.' He walked over to the gate in the corral.

He turned to the old man sitting in the chair, leaning against the shack, 'I thank you for putting my horses up and for the information. Sorry we got interrupted but, well, you can see how it is.'

The older man nodded but didn't say anything.

'Yeah, yeah, enough of this bullshit. Get your horses like I said,' Dutch growled, settling his feet and slightly crouching, his right hand hovering over his holstered pistol grip.

'Did you ever get up in the morning,' Nate

said to Dutch, 'and think maybe this just wasn't your day?'

As Dutch frowned and took a step or two closer, Nate settled his hat on his head, shrugged his shoulders and turned to the gate. Sliding the bottom rail to the left, he put one arm over the top rail at one end. Gripping it in his strong right hand, he lifted it up enough to clear the other side of the gate and quickly swung it around, catching Dutch in the stomach.

Grunting, the big man bent over, holding his middle with both hands. Nate took another grip on the ten-foot-long fence rail and swung again, this time hitting the man on the side of his head. Dutch flew back, coming straight up and, like a falling tree, straight back, landing flat. His breathing was nasal and loud, the steady sound of a man who was out cold.

'Wal,' Tex said with a chuckle, still not moving from his tilted chair. 'Can't say he didn't get a surprise.' Then after bringing the chair down on to its four legs, the old man slowly stood and walked over to look down at Dutch lying spread-eagled in the dust of the street.

'I guess ya best jump aboard that horse of yorn and light out. Old Dutch is gonna be madder than hell, he wakes up, don't ya know?'

Nate replaced the top rail. He took his horse's reins in his hand and walked over to stand beside the old man.

'Yeah, I suppose that'd be the smart thing to do,' he said. 'But I guess I'll stop by and see how Mrs Harmon is making out first. Keep an eye on my pack-horse, will you?'

'Hah! Leave it to a pretty young woman to mess up the mind of a man. Gonna get ya in big trouble. But sure, I'll watch your horse. That's what I do for a living. Cost ya two bits.'

Nate reached down, and unbuckled the gunbelt from the unconscious man. 'That should slow him down a mite. And I'm not looking for anything from Mrs Harmon. My plans call for me to winter somewhere in California.'

'Uh-huh. And the widow Harmon won't change anything, will she? Naw, same old story, young man, but you can't see it. Too young and dumb, don't ya know? Go ahead. I'll tell your friend here you lit out.'

Nate settled himself in the saddle and, with a wave and a squeeze of his knees, headed up the street toward the sheriff's office.

Nobody seemed to have seen the incident

at the corral, but then Nate figured it had happened too fast. He didn't remember planning it out, it just seemed to happen. When he first pushed the lower rail back it was just to get his pack-horse out. But knowing that was what Dutch wanted angered him and the next thing Nate knew, bam, the bigger man was flat on his back.

Stopping in front of the sheriff's office, Nate sat his horse and thought for a moment about the first time he'd seen her in Powell's saloon and store. Shaking his head, he dropped the reins over the hitching-rail, slung Dutch's gunbelt over his shoulder, and opened the door to the sheriff's office.

Sheriff Brickey wasn't alone. A woman in a loud-print dress was standing in front of the lawman, shaking her finger in his face. Nate's first thought was that she was wearing a big wooden barrel under a blue tent, a tent with yellow flowers all over it.

When the door opened, the woman turned to see who had interrupted her. The woman's finger remained in the air as if she didn't want to lose her place.

'Good morning, Nate,' the sheriff said with some relief in his voice.

'Is this the young cowboy who stuck his nose in where it didn't belong?' the woman demanded in a loud, angry voice.

The colorful barrel of a woman swung around, and Nate found himself the target of the lecturing finger. 'You'll be sorry you got in the way of the law, young man. People in this town don't appreciate interference from anyone, especially a stranger.' Her eyes seemed to be two small black marbles that someone had stuck in one of the bigger seams of her round face.

A mouth, tiny as the pointed little nose above it, was opening and closing so fast Nate could almost hear her little white teeth click as she loudly told him off. Short as she was round, the top of her head stopped just short of Nate's chin.

'Don't you stand there smiling down at me, you you...' Nate hadn't been aware he was smiling.

He turned to the sheriff while the woman tried to find the right words, and started to tell him about the fight at the corral. Before he could get a word out, though, she was back in business. Only now her finger was aimed at the lawman again.

'If you were any kind of law officer, Brickey, you'd arrest this man. He probably had something to do with the whole affair.'

Stepping right into the conversation, Nate

smiled apologetically. 'I didn't mean to interrupt, ma'am. Just wanted to drop this gun belt off to the sheriff,' he said, handing Dutch's heavy belt over.

'Where did you get this,' Brickey asked, visibly relieved to have something to do that didn't include the jabbering woman.

'Well, I took it off your deputy, Dutch,' Nate said.

'You what?' the woman yelped. 'Nobody could take anything from that man. A big, ugly, dirty brute, but nobody could take his gun unless he's dead. Sheriff,' she said, having obviously gotten her second wind, 'Sheriff, I insist you arrest this man. He had to have shot poor Mr Voles in the back to get his gunbelt. A person isn't safe with this kind free on the street.'

'Now, Mrs Runkle, we don't know that Dutch is even dead.' Looking past the woman, he asked once more, 'How did you get his gunbelt, young man.'

'Why, I just took it from him. He's down by the corral, just lying in the street. Was still breathing when I left him. I didn't want anyone to steal it while he slept, so I thought I'd bring it to you for safe keeping.' Nodding to the short round woman, he added, smiling, 'But you go ahead. I can wait until you are finished before explaining all about it.'

'I don't believe it for a minute. Sheriff, if you don't arrest him right now, the good women of this town will not be safe. I demand it.'

'No, Mrs Runkle,' said Brickey, shaking his head, 'I won't arrest him. At least, not until I find out if he broke a law. Now, if you will excuse me, I have some law business to clear up.'

'Law business. That's what I'm here for. Why have you let that thieving Harmon woman out of jail? She should be behind bars until the judge gets here. I'm told she is out, running free.'

Once again Sheriff Brickey shook his head. 'No, Mrs Runkle, she is not out running around free. She is in my custody. Happens I think having her at my house is better than in the jail. She'll be on hand when the judge gets here.'

'She ought to be run out of town; a common thief is all she is.' The round woman's face took on an almost delicate pink color as her voice climbed higher and became more strident. Nate quickly looked away to keep her from seeing his smile.

'The judge, when he gets here, will decide what to do with her,' Brickey said, 'we don't know she took your jewels, Mrs Runkle. She says she never saw them. Are you sure you didn't just mislay them someplace?'

'No! They disappeared when she left my home. After doing my duty and letting her stay in my home while she was burying her husband, that's the thanks I get. My mother's cameo brooch and pearl necklace that's been in my family for years – she's a thief and I want her in jail where she belongs!'

Heaving a big sigh the sheriff shook his head again. 'No, I won't put her in jail. Now you go about your business. I have things to do.' Firmly he grasped her arm and turned her toward the door. Nate quickly moved out of the way.

'All right,' she said, pulling her arm free. 'Throw me out of your office. But the good people of this town will hear about it. Election time is coming, you know.' Nate, holding the door, tipped his hat to her as she stamped out.

Wiping a handkerchief across his balding head, Sheriff Brickey sat down in the chair behind his desk and let out another big sigh.

'Too damn early in the day for that,' he said, looking at Nate as the younger man leaned against the wall. 'Now, what's this about your taking Vole's gun from him?'

Quickly Nate told him about Dutch's attempt to run him out of town. 'I thought it best to take his gun. Maybe you can hold it until I'm gone.'

Neither man spoke for a moment as the sheriff took a sack of tobacco from a pocket and deftly rolled a smoke. After offering the sack to Nate, he put it back in his pocket when the younger man shook his head.

'What's that all about, Sheriff, her claim that Mrs Harmon took her jewelry? And how come you sent someone like Dutch out to bring her back to town?'

The older man pushed himself up from the chair and walked over to the pot-bellied stove.

'Want a cup of coffee?' Nate nodded and took the thick white mug of steaming liquid that was offered.

'Old lady Runkle thinks she can scare me with talk about the "good people" of the town and elections. Hell, I agreed to take the job just to stop her husband from getting Dutch in the office. Don't think I'll do it again, though, even if I could get elected. Let the "good people" see how they like having that big fool for a sheriff.'

'Seems the Runkles just about run the town,' Nate said, almost making a question of the statement.

'Yeah. They came into town five, six years ago. Bought the bank from old man Adams. A good man, but old. Wanted to go back East. Had some family back there, I guess. Anyhow, after that Runkle just picked things up from people when, for one reason or another, they ran into money trouble.'

Sipping the hot, black coffee, the two men were silent as they thought about the way it always seemed to work. Having control of the money, you could buy the bank or the saloon. If you were a cowhand, you could only buy a drink or two in the saloon.

'Anyhow,' the sheriff went on almost sadly, 'as things turn out, the pair of them just about run the town. She runs the women and he runs the bank. And the irrigation ditch. And the saloon.'

Disgustedly, the older man got up to pour another cup of coffee. 'Oh, the people here, for the most part, are good people. They're just too interested in making a living, so they don't pay much attention to any other problems. Mostly, I guess they just don't have time to do more than mind their own business. For some folks it helps if there's someone to do their thinking for them.'

Nodding, Nate waited to see if the man

had anything more to add on the subject. When Brickey didn't go on, he took a sip of coffee and said quietly, 'And Mrs Harmon?'

'I don't know what that's all about. Sarah, that's her name. Was Sarah Noble before she married Jess Harmon. Her daddy died just about the time the Runkles came into town. Soon after Sarah up and married Jess. He'd been the ranch foreman. Then a couple weeks ago, Sarah brought Jess's body in. She'd found it at the bottom of one of those steep cap rock mesas. Must have been throwed when his horse spooked, I guess. Head was all soft and out of shape. She's a strong girl, though. She'd wrapped him in a blanket, piled him in a wagon, and brought him in.'

The lawman stopped for a minute, then, shaking his head, continued: 'Anyhow, she was strong, but once she got to town and turned her husband's body over to the undertaker, she fell apart. Couldn't stop crying. The Runkles offered to take her in. Wasn't right, Mrs Runkle said, for her to be alone in a hotel room. Jess was buried the next day and Sarah packed up and drove back home. It was a couple days later when the banker came to me, claiming Sarah had stolen his wife's jewelry.'

'And you sent Dutch out to bring her in?'

'Oh, gawd yes. Runkle was giving me a bad time, came in all hot and bothered, yelling that I had better go out and get her. I took a fall a few weeks ago and stove up my leg. I can't ride a saddle and sitting a wagon seat very long just kills me. So when Runkle offered to pay Dutch to go out for me, I guess I took the easy way out and let it happen. Damn fool thing that was. I wasn't thinking clear. Gave that idiot a badge, thinking it would keep him honest. Shoulda known better.'

Nate didn't say anything for a minute or two. 'But nothing happened, so I guess it's all right,' he then said softly. 'How is she today? Mrs Harmon, I mean.'

'Doesn't look like she slept much last night, wouldn't eat much breakfast this morning, either. She's very sad-looking.'

'Mind if I go talk with her?'

'Boy, you sure taking a big interest in her. Don't forget, that damn Dutch'll be looking for you,' Brickey said warningly.

'Not likely. I'll just talk with her. See if there's anything I can do. Then I'll be on my way south.'

'Guess it couldn't hurt any,' the sheriff

said, getting up and leading the way out of his office. 'I'll walk down with you so Ida won't be worried.'

CHAPTER 8

Harney had to laugh when he saw the kid, as he'd started to call him, use the fence rail to knock the bigger man down. At first he thought he was about to lose his only source for that gold, but the young man was pretty tricky. He ducked back in a doorway and watched as the kid took the big man's gunbelt and delivered it to the sheriff. Looking back at the old man at the corral, he decided to ask him some questions.

The two men left the main business district, walking down toward the river. Homes, mostly log-cabins and, for the most part, no bigger than two rooms, were scattered along the river bank. A couple of the larger ones were built of the same rough planks used in the construction of the town. These were set apart on a little rise overlooking a bend in the river.

It was to a larger than usual log-cabin the sheriff led Nate. Standing on a little point of land, the house was protected on one side by two large pine-trees. With all that had gone on since his arrival in town, Nate hadn't noticed the small forest of big trees growing in a scattered fashion along the river. Brickey walked across the porch, opened the front door and motioned Nate on in.

'Welcome to my home,' the lawman said before loudly calling his wife. 'Ida, we've company.'

The living-room was furnished with com-fortable-looking bent-willow easy-chairs covered with thick pillows. A ragrug covered the plank floor. A curtained door to the left probably led to a bedroom, Nate figured, and the open door opposite where the men stood had to be the kitchen.

'We're in the kitchen, Roy,' a woman's voice answered as she moved into the open doorway. A tall woman, her gray-streaked hair was pulled back into a tight bun at the back of her head. She had large brown eyes that smiled when she heard her husband introduce the man he had brought home.

'This is the young man who helped Mrs Harmon yesterday. Nate Ragan, my wife Ida.'

'How do you do, Mr Ragan. Sarah told us

what you did to help her at Powell's Store. I'm glad Roy brought you home. Would you like a cup of coffee?' Before Nate could answer, she moved to a large black iron cook-stove, picked up a heavy white cup and poured. 'I'll bet he's been giving you that stuff he drinks over at the jail. This at least is fresh-ground and fresh-brewed.'

Nate had stopped listening as she prattled on. Looking past the sheriff's wife, he saw Sarah Harmon watching him. She stood at a waist-high bench that ran along the back wall of the room. The bench contained a sink and the young woman had been washing up the morning's breakfast dishes. Soap-suds covered her arms as she turned, soapy plate in hand, when the men came into the room. A small smile brightened her face as her eyes found Nate.

'Hello, Mr Ragan,' Sarah said, putting down the plate and drying her hands.

'Here, Mr Ragan. Sit down here,' Mrs Brickey said, setting his cup on the square kitchen table. Her husband, a smile on his face, walked over to pour himself a cup of coffee.

Sarah Harmon was wearing a long dress of some soft blue pattern, Nate noticed. The material was smooth across her shoulders, which were squared, her back as straight as one who had spent much of her life on a horse. The dress was belted at her narrow waist, then fell away, softly draped across her rounded hips before falling in pleats to just above the tops of her shoes. All this Nate saw in a brief moment, before his eyes returned quickly to hers.

Blue. He remembered, her eyes were the deepest blue. Her mouth, bent upward at the corners in a smile, was more than the young man could stand. Quickly he dropped his eyes to the offered chair, his face growing warm. He removed his hat and sat down. The sheriff pulled a chair away from the table and seated himself also. Mrs Brickey filled two cups that were already on the table before seating herself. The young woman, after drying the soap from her hands, joined them.

'I want to thank you for helping me yesterday,' Sarah Harmon said. 'I hate to think what might have happened if you hadn't come along with us into town.'

Sheriff Brickey, whose head had been somewhat hanging, looked up at Nate. 'Don't know what I was thinking about, sending a man like that out there.'

'Now, Roy, what were you to do?' Mrs Brickey said, reaching out to put her hand on her husband's shoulder. 'How were you to know what might happen? After all, you certainly couldn't go.'

More to get her to look at him and to hear her speak again, Nate turned to Sarah Harmon. 'Where did the Runkles' charge come from, anyhow? Mrs Runkle was hammering at the sheriff about you're not being in jail already this morning. She certainly doesn't like you, does she?'

'I thought she did,' Sarah Harmon said quietly. Nate noticed that the face he had at first thought was round wasn't, but then he decided it really wasn't thin either. 'After I brought my husband's body to town, it was too late to head back to the ranch, so I decided to take a room at the hotel. Mrs Runkle wouldn't hear of it. Said I needed the comfort of another woman and invited me to stay at her house. I didn't want to, but couldn't think of a way to say no, so I ended up staying there.

'She was nice to me, I guess. I was very tired and went right to bed.'

'What did her husband have to say about your staying at his house,' the sheriff asked, taking a sip of the cooling coffee.

'Well, I don't recall him saying anything. He seemed to be quiet. Oh, he did ask one

73

time what my plans were. If I was going to sell the ranch.'

'How did your husband die,' Nate asked before he thought how nosy that might sound. As soon as he asked he knew he'd said the wrong thing. 'Ah, I'm sorry. It's not any of my business, and I have no right to remind you of it. Should just keep my mouth shut.'

'No,' the young woman said softly, looking into her coffee-cup. 'It'll be easier, I think, if I talk about it. Mr Runkle said he didn't agree, that I should keep it to myself. But somehow I think that'll only make the hurt last longer.'

'Yes, dear,' Mrs Brickey said in agreement. 'You really shouldn't keep it bottled up inside. But it would not be helpful to dwell on it, either.'

'No, I don't, really. Jess was up at the far end of the main canyon. He'd gone up there to check on the big ditch. He'd gone out early and I rode out about noon to take him a sandwich and a bottle of cold water from the well. I found his horse up on the cap rock and, as I looked around, I happened to see his body down at the bottom. His head was all bloody. I guess his horse had spooked and he'd fallen. I wrapped him in a blanket and put him in a ranch wagon to bring him to town.'

'That must have been hard,' Nate said sympathetically.

'It had to be done, Mr Ragan. It took most of the afternoon to get him into town. I guess it was lucky it happened so close to the road.' As she told the story her voice had softened. While her eyes were open, those at the table knew she was not seeing them. She was quietly reliving that awful afternoon's experience.

Nate, still uncomfortable to have brought the sad memory back to her, tried to think of something that would get her mind on to some other subject.

'Nate. My front name is Nate, not Mr.' He waited a minute until she nodded and then went on: 'It's too bad it happened. Is there anyone at the ranch, taking care of things while you're in town?' he asked.

'Yes, we've got three men on full time. But I don't suppose they know where I am or what happened. They were all out moving cattle when that Voles man came out and brought me back. He wouldn't let me leave a note, he wouldn't even let me change into town clothes.' Anger came back to her voice as she remembered her arrest.

'I was working in the garden, wearing old clothes when he rode up. He sat there just staring at me. When I ignored him, he told me I was coming back to town. The sheriff wanted to talk to me, he said. I asked what for and he told me I was under arrest. That shocked me and the next thing I knew he had handcuffed me. I don't remember much about the ride until we got to Powell's Store and you got me a drink of water,' she looked once more directly at Nate.

Once again he felt his face warm up. 'Well, uh, maybe I could ride out and talk to your men, tell them what happened and where you are,' he said without thinking, just saying the first thing that came to him.

'Oh, I couldn't ask you to do that,' she said, brightening. 'Although I should let them know. But you've already done so much for me. Riding in yesterday to keep that dirty man away was wonderful.'

Nate quickly looked down at his coffee-cup. He missed seeing the brief smile pass between the sheriff and his wife.

'Well, I was coming this way anyhow. But,' he quickly added, 'I could ride out this afternoon and give your men any messages you want. Don't seem like you'll be going back out to the ranch for a while.'

'The circuit judge won't be here for another week or so,' the sheriff said. 'You'll have to stay with us till then, I guess.'

'I'm sorry to put you out. I could go back to the jail. It would be less work for you, Mrs Brickey,' Sarah said slowly.

'Now, hush that talk. I would not let Roy lock you up. Why, the time will go by so fast, and it'll do you good to be away from the ranch for a while.'

Turning to Nate, Sarah smiled. 'All right. It would help if you rode out and told Hank and the boys where I am and why. They'll probably be working somewhere near the river or along one of the ditches in the big pasture. Hank Lakewood, he's the foreman. He knows what needs to be done with the stock but he'll start to worry when they come in and don't find me at the ranch.'

Mrs Brickey offered to make a couple sandwiches for Nate to take with him, after glancing once more at her husband. Catching the glint in his eye, she turned her back quickly to her task, not wanting either of the young people to see her smile.

CHAPTER 9

Nate untied his horse and climbed into the saddle, then realized that he didn't know where the Crooked River ranch was. It would not sit well, he decided, if he went back and to ask directions. Certainly the old man at the town's corral would help him.

Riding slowly back through town, he watched warily for any sign of Dutch Voles. Running into the big man wasn't something he looked forward to now. He kept a firm hand on the reins, poised to jab the spurs to his horse if necessary.

Nate arrived at the corral without seeing anyone he knew. He swung down and, holding his reins, hunkered down near the porch where Tex was sitting.

'Hey, old-timer, I see my friend Dutch woke up. Or did you get tired of looking at him and drag him out of the street?'

'Boy, ya sure got your nerve, riding right down the street. Yeah, he woke up right after ya left. Madder than hell, too. Cussing and carrying on, swearing he was going to find

ya. Gonna shoot first and talk later, he said.'
Tex spat a stream of tobacco-juice into the dirt of the street.

'Well, guess that'll have to wait for another day. But I've got a question.'

'Hope this time we can just talk without being interrupted by anyone with a gun. Makes too much excitement for an old man, don't ya know?'

Looking down the street toward the saloon, Nate smiled. 'I'm going to ride out to Mrs Harmon's place. She asked me to take a message to her hired hands, telling them where she is and what happened to her. Can you set me in the right direction? She figures they'll be working the herd somewhere in the big pasture, she said.'

'Yeah, I guessed something like that. Pretty girl'll be trouble every time, don't ya know? Ah, well, I can remember how it was, don't think I can't.

'Wal, there's two ways ya can go. See that hill over there to the east?' He pointed to the bare knob of a hill Nate had noticed when riding into town. It looked to be a mile or so east of the little town.

'Yeah.'

'Wal, that's Pilot Butte. If ya was to ride that trail there,' he said pointing along a well-traveled trail eastward, toward the hill, 'it'll take ya east clear across the desert country, if ya was to follow it all the way. About five, six miles from town, though, a wagon trail takes off to the north, down off the cap rock and alongside the Crooked River. The ranch house is some mile or so along the river. Gotta watch out and not get off to the south of the trail along there, looks pretty good, but changes real fast into dry desert. Hell, even the junipers won't grow out there. No water and the sand is fine. Shifts a lot, they say, and your trail'll simply disappear.'

Nate noticed that as the man talked, he was keeping an eye on the goings-on up the street.

'The other way,' the old man continued, 'is back the way ya come, back through town, along that trail sorta north and east to Powell's Store. Keep on that way and you'll end up in Shaniko.'

'Yeah,' Nate nodded, 'that's the way I rode in.'

Tex spat a tobacco-stream and nodded. 'OK, once ya drop off the cap rock, follow the river back southward. That's probably where the crew is working. The bigger pastures are at that end. That's the quickest if you're going horseback. Riding a wagon, though, ya might want to take the east trail around Pilot Butte.' The old man spat another stream and then, digging a flat package of thick-cut tobacco from a pocket, he broke off a goodly amount and shoved it back into his mouth.

Nate watched as the old man got the chew settled between his jaw and cheek. It was probably impolite to ask where the last chew of the black, oily-looking tobacco had gone. Probably something he really didn't want to know, anyhow, Nate thought.

Once his tobacco was comfortable, Tex, looking up at the sky, said: 'This late in the morning, ya had better be figuring on being gone over night. It's a good three- or four-hour ride each way.'

'I guess that's what I'll do,' Nate agreed, then, looking at the old man, went on: 'Guess I'll be heading on to California after I do this favor for Sarah ... huh, Mrs Harmon.'

'Sure ya will. Oh, by the way, there was a fella stop by and ask about ya.'

'Not another friend of the banker, was it?'

'Nope. A stranger. Older, and looking like he might be some kind of storekeeper or something. Not someone you'd likely notice, medium tall and thinly built.' Tex thought a minute, 'Was wearing a dark suit and a black narrow-brimmed hat. The suit all looking shiny like it was old. Wanted to know who you were. I told him as far as I knew, just someone riding through on his way to California.' He laughed.

'Well, I guess it isn't something for me to worry about. Seems like I got enough worry lately. Don't need any more.'

Nate swung into the saddle, turned to wave to the old man, and took off. Thinking it would probably not help to run into Voles, he skirted around the edge of town and headed out across the sagebrush to connect with the trail towards Powell's Store.

CHAPTER 10

Dutch and the banker, Runkle, had watched the young cowboy ride by earlier, as he was heading toward the corral.

'He can't hit me like he did and get away with it,' Voles growled. The two men had been sitting in Runkle's second-floor office over the saloon when Nate came up from the sheriff's house, to ride seemingly un-afraid down the main street. 'I'll kill the son-of-a-bitch,' he said. He jumped up from the chair he'd been lounging in and headed for the door.

'Oh, sit down,' the portly banker said, watching the horseman ride by. Slowly he rose from behind his desk and moved to a curtained window to watch the street's activities. He turned and stared at Dutch for a moment, thinking, planning.

'You had your chance at that meddler, now you've got other things to do.'

'Hell, he hit me when I wasn't looking. I'm not going to let him walk away from that. I ain't through with him.'

'If you'd been paying attention, he wouldn't have had the opportunity to hit you,' the banker said sneeringly. 'But forget him. I want you to get your horse and ride out to the Harmon ranch.'

'What the hell? That's a long ride. What do I have to ride all the way back out there for? The girl's in town.'

'Quit bitching. I'm paying you to ride out there, that's why. Now listen to me.' Runkle returned to his desk and sat down. He took a small polished-wood box from a drawer, opened it and took a cloth-covered package out and handed it to the bigger man.

'Take this out to the ranch. Leave it on a

table or shelf in the living-room, or better yet, in the widow's bedroom. Whatever you do, don't let anyone see you.'

'Why the hell do I gotta ride clear out there? I coulda left it there yesterday when I got the girl.'

'Damn it, Dutch. Don't you go arguing with me. You like taking my money. Now dammit, you can earn it.' The banker got up from the desk once again and walked back to the window overlooking the street. He liked to watch people, see who was going where. It gave him a sense of power. Still facing the closed window, Runkle smiled, a hard, cold smile.

'One way or the other, I'm going to have that ranch,' he said, almost to himself. 'When the sheriff finds these jewels he'll have all the proof that she did steal them from my wife. She'll have to make a deal with me then, sell me the ranch or go to jail.'

'Hell, why go to all that work? Just go take it. Nobody's gonna argue.'

'No, I want it legally. When she sees the evidence is all against her and she runs the chance of going to prison, I'll offer to drop the charges if she'll leave the territory. After signing her ranch over to me, of course.'

Dutch, watching from the comfort of his

chair, saw his boss stiffen at something he saw. The banker didn't say anything as he watched Nate start his circle around town.

'Dutch, take the south trail out of town. Cut back behind the hotel and ride out a ways so that damn old man down at the corral don't see you, then pick up the trail farther out. And make sure nobody sees you when you come back into town, too.'

'Now why do I want to go to all that trouble? Dammit, Mr Runkle, you're making it extra hard on me.' Thinking a minute, Dutch figured that now was a good time to make his pitch. 'Another thing, saying you get the Harmon ranch, what do I get for all this work and riding I'm doing? It's gotta be worth a lot more than the piddlin' little I've seen so far.'

Runkle turned to look at the big man. The banker frowned as he saw the greed in Dutch's eyes. 'I have the bank to run and the irrigation project to expand. Don't worry, you'll be taken care of. I'll need someone I can trust to ramrod the ranch, won't I? Now, you better get going,' he said, picking up his flat-crowned hat and setting it squarely on his head. 'I'll go talk to the sheriff. Get back as soon as you can. Hell, he may deputize you again, to go out to search the widow's house for the jewels.'

Chuckling at the thought, he let Dutch out the back door and then once more stood at the window, looking out over the town. His town.

Runkle thought about his plan and smiled. Of course, he decided, Voles could become a problem. His man, the banker decided, was getting some big ideas. When this is over, he thought, I'll have to do something about him. Deep in thought, he didn't hear his portly wife come up behind him. Catching the movement out of the corner of his eye, he whirled around, cursing.

'Damn it, woman. You shouldn't come sneaking up behind me like that,' he said angrily, his voice rising.

'John,' she said ignoring his outburst. Her voice was soft, which made it seem to her husband, more threatening. 'Why did you give that bastard my jewelry? That wasn't what you told me you'd do when I gave them to you.'

'Now, honey.' Runkle softened his voice, working to keep his words calm. 'Things have changed a little, but nothing for you to worry about. Dutch'll leave the jewels at the Harmon ranch. I'll force the sheriff into going out and making a search. He'll discover them among the widow's personal things and my case against her is sealed tight. You'll get your stuff back and I can make a deal to buy her out.'

'Oh, John, you've been making big plans ever since we married and every time something has gone wrong. I'm worried. This time it's my jewelry that I'm afraid of losing.'

'There is no reason to fret, dear. This time—'

'This time,' she interrupted him, her voice slightly stronger, overriding his. 'This time. I heard that last time when you lost nearly half of the money Daddy left me with your scheming. And we nearly got run out of that dinky little town, if you recall.'

'This is different. Look,' he hated it when he heard the pleading tone of his words, 'once the ranch is mine ... ours, we'll send a couple hundred head north to the market in Shaniko and travel over to Oregon City and go shopping. You'll bring back enough new dresses it'll keep the town's old biddies bent over their sewing-needles for a year.'

Smiling, he held out his arms invitingly to his wife. Instead of coming into the offered hug as he expected, she continued to stand, staring at him.

'John, if anything goes wrong ... if I lose

my mother's jewels and the last of Daddy's money, well, it'll be the final straw.' Her voice was still soft, but there was a hard tone that caused the banker to draw back.

'Now, sweetheart–'

'Don't forget. The bank, the irrigation system and that smelly saloon you're so proud of were all bought with my Daddy's money. You wouldn't be the big man you think you are without it. Sometimes I think you forget that fact.'

'You'll have it all back,' he said, losing patience and letting his words carry the authority needed to put her back in her place. 'When this is all over, you'll have it all back and more. This is a sure-fire deal.'

She looked at him for a moment longer, then turned wordlessly and left the room. Maybe, he thought, watching her walk away, he'd have to do something about her after this was all over. Shaking his head with disgust, he went to the door and watched as she waddled down the hallway, going heavily down the back stairs.

CHAPTER 11

When Nate's stomach gave notice, he started looking for a place out of the early-afternoon sun. Since leaving the little community, he hadn't seen anything more than the rolling hills, all covered with seemingly identical juniper trees. Closer to the ground, the dusty gray of sagebrush shared the sandy-looking soil with clumps of rabbit-grass.

To the west, over his left shoulder, Nate could see the snow-capped mountains of the Cascade Range. Turning to look behind him, he could easily spot the rounded hill Tex had called Pilot Butte. Ahead there were endless miles of country the same as that he was riding through.

Sagebrush and clumps of juniper trees, he was sure, wasn't the kind of country for him. In his mind's eye he saw himself riding through new country farther south, stopping here and there to fish in the creeks, rivers and high mountain lakes he found. He had no exact idea when he would get to the end of the trip. He never thought of that.

He simply thought of going to California as if that was enough.

Harney had watched as Ragan rode out of town. The kid had talked with that old guy down at the corral before riding north through town. Maybe he was heading back up the trail to look for the saddle-bag of gold that Calhoun had hidden. As he rushed back to where he had his horse tied, he decided be couldn't take a chance. He would have to follow Ragan. Hell, maybe this was his opportunity to get the young man off by himself for a little talk. Yeah. Maybe.

Nate was riding and dozing in the saddle when his horse came to an abrupt halt, rearing a little. 'What the hell....' he yelled, then settling the horse down he looked down to find a man holding the horse's bridle in one hand and a revolver in the other.

'Man, you must be hard up to think you'll get anything robbing me,' he said. Then remembering the description of the man Tex had told him about, Nate changed his mind ... this wasn't just any old robbery. 'Hey, what the hell are you after?'

'Don't matter. Just get down off that horse and be quick about it.' The thin man holding the gun was older than he had at first looked. Deep wrinkles marred the dark sun-blackened skin of his face. 'You're about to tell me what my old partner told you before he died.'

Old partner... Nate realized this had to be the man who'd taken those shots at him back along that little creek out of Shaniko. Who did the sheriff say he was? Harney, Amos Harney.

'Now what makes you think he told me anything? Hells bells, he was gasping his last when I found him. Some partner you turned out to be. Tell me,' Nate asked, relaxing a bit in the saddle, 'how much gold did you two find? Enough to shoot your partner?'

Stepping back a few feet, Harney motioned with his Colt. 'C'mon. You'll get to talk all you want. Now get outa that saddle.'

Nate sat still a moment, then, taking both reins in one hand and putting the other on the saddle horn, he jabbed his heels into his horse's side. Surprised, the animal bolted and with Nate lying as low as he could and still kicking his heels, made a mad dash away leaving the old man standing in the trail behind him.

CHAPTER 12

Dutch Vole reached the cap rock over-looking the upper Crooked River and pulled up. Remembering he wasn't to be seen, he took a slow look in all directions. Far below, he could see one of the rock-diversion dams old man Noble had built. The river wasn't very deep at that point and it made a good place to ford the stream.

At about the same time as Voles was turning back to the trail down off the rim rock to the river, Nate was miles downstream, fording the same river at the shallows near Powell's Store. After bringing his horse to a stop and letting him blow, he'd watched to make sure the old man wasn't following behind. Nate shook his head. If that ambushing idiot knew how little his partner had told him, he wouldn't believe it. Better to keep an eye out for the old duck. Glancing toward the long, low building, Nate decided he had no real reason to stop and rode on by. He turned along a well-defined trail and followed the river south. Unlike on top of the rim rock, the land down here had been cleared off. Riding along the edge of a broad, flat basin he noticed that the grass was no longer the clumps of bunchgrass he had been riding through, hut good rich stock feed.

Nate found the three-man crew late in the afternoon, working over a small, hot fire. The handles of half a dozen branding-irons stuck out of the fire. Nate sat his horse and watched as one cowboy, riding a small, fast piebald, roped a bawling calf and pulled it, fighting all the way, from the fifty or so head corralled in a makeshift rope pen. A second man quickly grabbed the calf by the tail and head and dumped the animal on its side. The third cowboy, wearing heavy leather gloves, grabbed the handle of one of the red-hot branding-irons and quickly burned the brand into the right hip of the calf. The second man looked up after freeing the mounted man's lasso and letting the calf jump up to escape back toward his corralled mother.

'Howdy,' the man said, standing slowly, brushing at his dirt-stained canvas pants as Nate rode up. He took a red handkerchief from a back pocket, removed his shapeless wide-brimmed hat and wiped the sweat from his face, never taking his eyes off Nate.

With his hat off, Nate could see he was older than he'd first appeared. His face, sun-darkened from halfway down his forehead and dead-white above that line, was deeply wrinkled. A large, hooked nose separated black eyes hooded under thick eyebrows.

'Howdy,' Nate answered, letting his glance take in the three men now facing him. 'I'm looking for the Harmon spread.'

'Wal,' the older man said, 'You've found it. Pull up a chair, we'll be done here in another hour or two.' He dropped his hat back on his head and turned to grab the reins from the dusty pinto. That cowboy picked up the leather gloves dropped by the man by the fire who turned to be ready to wrestle the next calf on to its side.

No one spoke as the three men worked, each doing his job, the three working like a well-oiled machine.

Nate sat back and watched the rhythm of the men. After the hot iron had marked three more squalling calves, he asked the man at the fire, 'Mind if I rope a few? My horse has been getting pretty lazy, lately.' Nate wasn't sure whether the horse he had got from James Clarke back in Shaniko knew how to cut out a calf, but most did and so far the animal had seemed willing.

'Can you use that throw rope?' the man asked, pointing to the lasso coiled and tied to Nate's saddle.

'Some,' Nate answered.

'Wal, you could give Hank a break. Don't suppose he'd mind too much.'

Hank didn't say anything as Nate shook out his loop and rode slowly into the corralled herd. With a quick twist of his right wrist, Nate sent the small, perfectly formed loop at the hind-feet of a brown-and-white yearling.

Either the calf heard the rope, or maybe saw it coming. It gave a jump to get away, but it was too slow. The lasso, perfectly timed, looped around its hind legs and Nate's horse, without missing a step, pulled up and turned back toward the fire.

Hank grudgingly nodded his approval and pulled his horse out of the dusty rope pen. He hooked one leg over his saddle horn, took a sack of tobacco from a shirt-pocket and slowly fashioned a cigarette.

By the time the last calf had made the trip to the branding-fire each of the men had taken their turn to be relieved and had enjoyed a smoke.

They broke down the temporary rope corral and tied all their gear on the back of a pack-horse, then the fire was quickly covered with dirt and stomped out.

'Said you was looking for the Harmon ranch, didn't you?' the man who had handled most of the actual branding said. Younger than the others, he was tall, about six inches taller than Nate. Sandy hair, sweat-soaked and looking in need of cutting, hung from under a flat-topped hat that had once been black. Dirt and sweat-salt had turned all but the edges of the brim gray. Watery blue eyes watched Nate as he asked the question.

'Mind saying what for?'

'Nope,' Nate said as he retied his catch rope to his saddle. 'Was asked by Miz Harmon to come out and tell her crew what's happening.'

Nate heard his words and realized he had lost his city speech and was talking with the same drawl as the men used.

At the mention of Mrs Harmon all three men stopped what they were doing and waited. Again, all eyes were on Nate. Suddenly, the three didn't look so friendly any more.

'She's been arrested,' Nate said, quietly.

'What you talking about?' the older man asked. 'Why would anyone arrest Miz Harmon?'

Slowly, Nate explained what had taken

place over the last few days, giving them the bare information that the banker in Farewell Bend had accused her of theft. They cussed and frowned at that, but Nate noticed they no longer looked at him with black eyes.

'So she asked you to come tell us,' the one named Hank said. 'Why you? What business is this to you?'

'I just happened along. Heading to California when I ran into that Voles fella while he was wearing the badge, taking Miz Harmon into town. I didn't like the looks of the man, so I trailed along into town.'

'Hell, if it's that Dutch Voles you're talking about, he ain't no lawman. He's just a would-be bad man. Works for old banker Runkle now and again,' the third man said.

Nate nodded in agreement. 'My name's Nate Ragan,' he said and waited.

'Yeah. Wal, I'm Hank, sorta acting foreman. The old fart there is Carl, only we call him Curly since he started losing his purty black hair that the women over at Sadie's like so much.' Pointing to the youngest of the three, Hank said his name was Lee.

Lee stood about five foot five and looked to weigh about 200 pounds. Stocky and hard-muscled, Nate saw, deciding he didn't want him for an enemy. After he'd shook hands all round, Hank, who had done all the talking for the crew, asked Nate if he wanted to ride in with them and spend the night at the bunkhouse.

'We been out three – four days, finishing up the branding. Miz Harmon wants to take a small herd up to Shaniko soon. 'Course, don't know if she wants to do that, now, have to talk to her about it, I guess.'

'Wal, I don't guess anything's changed,' the one called Curly said. 'She's still gotta pay off that note Jess gave Runkle, don't she?'

'Now, that ain't business of yourn,' Hank said quietly.

'I 'spect she's got a lot more on her mind than selling a herd,' Lee said, his voice almost as soft as Hank's.

The ranch hands rode alongside the river, then left the big basin only to pass by a narrow opening in a bluff and into another, smaller meadow.

'All the range in these pockets?' Nate asked.

'No,' Hank said. 'The home ranch is on up the river a piece, but back to the north of where you found us it spreads out into the prettiest flat land you ever did see. Most of it was claimed by old man Noble, and what wasn't can't be used without his water. He cleared all along the river down to about

Powell's Store, and then back along a couple good-sized creeks and into the flats.'

Nate watched and, from the cattle he saw, judged the ranch to be in very good financial shape. Most of the value would be on the hoof, but from what he knew of cattle and the need for beef in the gold-fields of California, the Harmon ranch had all the signs of being profitable.

CHAPTER 13

Voles had simply opened the front door and walked into the ranch house. The ride from town had taken a little longer than he'd figured. Shouldn't have wasted so much time thinking about being seen and dreaming about ramrodding a place like this, he said to himself as he stopped to look around the living-room.

The big man had never run a ranch before, had not even spent many days working on one. But that didn't even cross his mind. Hell, he thought, anyone can tell a good crew what to do. He'd tell them and they'd sure as hell do it, he thought, smiling.

He had plenty experience with that as a kid, having had to listen to his father yelling and giving out orders.

Now, he thought, older and smarter, he was about to become the foreman of the ranch on the Crooked River.

Looking around for a place to put the jewelry, he let his eyes take in the room. After all, he'd be living here soon. The living-room was full of heavy, hand-made pine furniture, making it look smaller than it really was. A stone fireplace, big enough to roast a calf in, filled the entire far wall. On the opposite end of the room, through an open door, Dutch could see a large kitchen table and the corner of a cast-iron stove.

A second door directly across the room was closed, and when the big man opened it, he found a large bedroom. That would be the best place for a woman to leave a neck-lace, he decided. A dresser, its top cluttered with tiny colorful bottles of things Dutch could only imagine a use for, seemed likely. He dropped the cameo brooch and necklace among the clutter, started to turn away, then stopped.

He glanced back over his shoulder, as if expecting someone to come into the bed-room, then he slowly, carefully and quietly pulled out one dresser-drawer after another until he found what he was looking for. Slowly he ran his hands over the missing woman's soft, silky, undergarments. Feeling them gently with the tips of his fingers, he was just beginning to smile and relax when, as if awakening from a dream, he was yanked awake. What if someone came riding up and spotted his horse?

Quickly he closed the drawers and hurried out to the front door, which he had left open. Carefully, not showing himself, he looked toward the barn and bunkhouse. Then, as he walked out to his horse, he once again slowly searched all around. Nothing.

But that didn't mean much, he decided. He'd better get his butt out of there. He settled his hat on his head, made sure the front door was closed, just as he had found it, and swung aboard his horse.

Reining back, he rode out the way he had come, soon gaining cover in a small grove of trees that had been planted on a slight ridge above the house. He stopped in that cover and looked back toward the buildings. Raising his eyes, he looked down the valley beyond and saw four horsemen riding in. Luck was with him.

Hidden among the trees, he watched as

the riders came into the yard, unsaddled and turned their horses into a pole corral. They were too far away, and Voles couldn't make out who they were. He probably wouldn't know them anyhow, he decided, just part of the Harmon crew.

Well, he thought as he watched the men wash up at a basin outside the long log bunkhouse, he didn't know who they were, but when he took over they'd certainly know who he was.

He turned and rode up the river, making the top of the rim rock just as the sun began to set behind the snow-capped mountains far to the west.

Nate shared the ranch hands' simple meal, cooked over a black stove that obviously served to heat the crew's living-quarters in winter. After dinner, a couple hands of pinochle were played. The men were in their bunks and snoring a short time later.

Up with the sun, after a quick breakfast, Nate sat in the morning sun drinking a cup of coffee. He watched as the three men rode out. Good men, he said to himself, relaxing against the bunkhouse wall. Their loyalty to Mrs Harmon was as strong as a rock, and for anyone not part of the ranch, they wouldn't give much more than a brief nod of recognition. But once they accepted the fact he was working in the best interests of the boss lady, they accepted him as one of themselves.

Alone, he casually looked around the yard. He noticed how well-kept things were. The peeled-pole corrals were not chewed through and there wasn't a weed to be seen anywhere. Flowers grew along the front porch of the main house, making a colorful border, separating the yard from the structure. Someone would have to carry water to those plants regularly, they wouldn't last long in the dry air and hot sun without it. Something a woman like Sarah would be sure to do.

The peeled-pine logs of the large main house glistened in the bright morning sun. Taking his nearly empty coffee cup, he walked over to the corral, deciding he'd take a look around before starting the long, dry ride back to town. It would be good, he decided, to get on his way south, out of this dry land.

Nate decided he'd ride out and look at the dams that made the ranch's irrigation system work on his way back to town. But first, he'd get the last of the morning's coffee. With the heavy mug filled with strong black coffee, he strolled toward the main house, then stopped abruptly. Hoof-prints and a pile of horse-droppings were clear evidence that someone had been to the house quite recently.

Hank had said that the crew had been out working the range for the past three or four days. Nobody, as far as he knew, had been here since Voles had taken Mrs Harmon away. Gently kicking the droppings with the toe of his boot, Nate figured they were not more than a day or so old.

Walking in a circle, Nate saw where someone, a man judging from the boot size, had got off the horse, and tied it to the porch railing. From the single pile of manure, he figured the horse had been tied to the railing for no long time, maybe less than an hour. Other traces showed where the visitor had later ridden out, southward, the same direction that Nate had decided to take when leaving the ranch.

Nate climbed up on to the porch and tried the front door. Finding it unlocked, he stepped inside. He placed the coffee cup carefully on the floor, let his hand drop to the butt of his holstered gun, and quickly checked out each room. Nothing seemed to be out of the ordinary or out of place. Everything was clean, although a little dusty, but in place.

Why, he asked himself, would anyone ride up to the house and tie his horse for an hour or so? Walking around the living-room, he looked closely at everything. Nothing seemed to be broken and the film of dust that covered things had not been disturbed. Whoever it had been, he didn't appear to be a thief.

Slowly, carefully, Nate gave the kitchen and bedroom the same inspection. It was in the bedroom that he noticed something out of place. One of the dresser-drawers wasn't closed completely. Well, Mrs Harmon might have left it like that. That's strange, he thought, here at her ranch, even in my mind I call her Mrs Harmon. In town, or riding out it had been Sarah.

Standing at the dresser, he thought about that. Oh, boy, he thought, you're doing too much thinking for a man on his way to California. As he let his eyes roam over the collection of bottles and knick-knacks on top of the dresser, he spotted the necklace.

'Whoa,' he said out loud. What was it the banker's wife had said Mrs Harmon had stolen? 'A pearl necklace and a cameo brooch'. Just like those sitting there among Mrs Harmon's pretties.

He reached out to pick up the jewelry but

stopped before touching them. They were clean, free of dust. Everything on the dresser top had that same thin film of dust, except the necklace and brooch. That meant that they had been recently placed there. Now I wonder, he frowned, why would someone leave them here in plain view?

Thinking a bit, he picked them up and dropped them in a shirt-pocket, which he buttoned carefully. He picked up his coffee cup, turned and left the house, carefully closing the door after him.

He cleaned up the coffee-pot and his cup and quickly rolled his bedding. He went to the corral, caught his horse and saddled up. As he rode back by the house he followed the tracks left by the unknown rider. Some-one knew some answers and Nate was of a mind to ask questions.

Nate didn't hurry as he rode back toward Farewell Bend, but kept his horse at a steady mile-eating trot. Before leaving the valley, he had stopped and spent some time inspecting one of the dams and the ditch that made the ranch viable. The slow-moving river flowed out of a straight-sided gorge, the walls on each side being black, rough rock that had once been molten volcanic lava. Over the millions of years, after the lava had cooled and hardened, the river had slowly cut its way until today the top of the flow was hundreds of feet above the moving water.

Old man Noble had started his main ditch just outside the chasm. Side ditches, smaller tributaries of the larger main ditch, carried water to the individual pastures. It was a well-planned system, simple but not easily or quickly constructed. Evidence of hard labor was seen along every foot of every ditch. Noble had been a real hard worker, Nate thought.

At last, having seen enough and not wanting to waste any more time, Nate once again took up the reins, following the trail taken by the unknown horseman. Any sign of the horse and rider had completely disappeared in the flinty lava rock long before the young cowboy reached the wagon trail that stretched to those ranches far to the east or west, back to the small community on the Deschutes River. It didn't matter, Nate thought, both he and the nameless rider had only one way to go, back to Farewell Bend.

CHAPTER 14

Nate rode up to the town corral just as the sun went down. Slowly he stretched his tired muscles and unsaddled. After giving his horse a rub-down and a forkful of hay, he drew back the pole gate and put his horse into the corral for the night.

Quietly he took his place, back against the old man's shed, and let his muscles slowly relax. First, he decided, he would enjoy sitting on something that didn't move under him. He would get some dinner and then report on his day to Sarah. Aha, he thought, back in town and she's 'Sarah' again.

'Wal, see ya made it back,' Tex said, walking up to claim his chair. 'Ya get your business taken care of, did ya?'

'I guess. That's a good size spread she's got there. Couple three good cowboys to work it, too.'

'So, ya met Hank and the boys, did ya? Yeah, they're the salt of the earth, as the saying goes. Hell on wheels when someone so much as looks cross-eyed at Miz Harmon, though,' he said, watching the young man's face closely.

'I suppose,' Nate said carelessly.

Neither said anything for a while, both looking up the street toward the business part of town. Some of the buildings were dark already, others well-lit with kerosene-lanterns out front.

'Wal, I guess you're back to riding off to California, huh?'

'Maybe in the morning,' Nate said.

'Yeah, I figured. Ya did your favor for the widow woman, didn't ya? No reason to hang around, then. And don't forget, there's that trick ya pulled on that bad man Voles. He'll not be forgetting it, don't ya know? Yeah, you'd better ride out early tomorrow.'

'Well, we'll see. By the way, you didn't see anyone ride in late yesterday, did you?' Nate asked innocently as he could, but watched the old wrangler closely.

'Didn't, but I don't see everyone. Didn't see ya ride in tonight, even. Who was ya expecting?'

'Don't know, but someone was at the Harmon ranch house before me. Probably late yesterday. Just wondered who it was.'

Nate rose slowly and stretched again. 'Guess I'll go get some supper and a good night's sleep. Probably come back and sleep in the hay again tonight.'

'Sure, same price as last time. Just don't wake me up when ya head out in the mornin'.'

'You sure are working hard to get me out of town. Why would I be leaving so early that you'd still be asleep?'

'Wasn't thinking about that trip to California yer always talking about. Nope, I hear the sheriff is going to ask ya to ride back out to the Harmon place to look for the banker's jewelry. Old man Runkle started working on getting Sheriff Brickey to ride out, but he cain't do that, not with his leg stove up. Hear Runkle wants Voles to go along, to protect his interest, don't ya know? And Miz Harmon suggested that you go along to watch him, protect her interests. Now, if'n you're tired of all that riding back and forth, you'd better get an early start, tomorrow.'

Nate looked over at the old man and shook his head, tiredly. 'Guess I'll have to go along, if she asked me to.'

Tex snorted. 'Thought ya would. Like I say, just don't wake me up in the morning.'

Nate turned and walked up the street to the Miners' saloon and supper. Before he got there, though, he stopped. Looking down toward the river at the trappers' cabin, he stood thinking. Guess I need a clean shirt out of my saddle-bags, he said silently. He turned to the log cabin, kicked the door open and, feeling for his hanging pack, found a stub of candle. By the flickering light he pulled a clean shirt from the pack and shoved the dirty one in in its place – after taking the jewelry from the pocket of the dirty one.

He found a small square of soft cloth in the pack, in which he carefully wrapped the necklace and brooch, tying the package with a short piece of string. He looked around and found one of the larger areas of grass and dried mud chinking between two logs. Carefully he pulled the mud wad free and shoved the wrapped package into the cavity. Then he replaced the chinking.

He carefully brushed out any sign of his hiding-place, replaced the candle in the pack, took the clean shirt and walked down to the river. After washing up in the cold, swift-moving water, he put on the shirt and walked on up town for his dinner.

After a meal of steak, beans, home-made bread and coffee, the young man felt ready for anything. Until, that was, the door to Sheriff Brickey's home opened to his knock and he found himself looking into the deepest blue eyes he could ever remember seeing.

'Hello, Nate,' Sarah said softly. She stepped aside and welcomed him into the house. 'Won't you come in. The sheriff and Mrs Brickey are waiting to talk to you. They're in the kitchen.'

'Come in, young man,' Sheriff Brickey said with a smile. He pushed a chair away from the round oak table in the center of the large, warm kitchen. Brickey remained seated, but his wife had jumped up as Nate walked into the friendly-feeling room, and had a coffee cup out, ready to pour.

'Would you like some honey to put in your coffee,' she asked, pouring the thick, white cup full of the hot, black liquid. 'Have you had any dinner yet? There is some stew left over, it's probably still hot.'

'Ida,' the older man said gently, 'leave the man time to get settled. I swear,' he said, looking at Nate, 'these women have just been acting strange all day. If one wasn't out on the porch looking down the street, the other one was. What they were looking for, I sure don't know.'

'Roy, you just stop that,' the woman said. 'You know we were watching for this young man ever since he left yesterday.' Turning to

Nate, she went on: 'That Voles man rode out just after you, only he took the southern road. We were afraid he was going out to find you.'

'Well, I didn't run across him,' Nate said, then to Sarah, he went on: 'But I did find your crew. They have things pretty well under control, I'd say.'

'Oh, thank you. I didn't want them to worry.' Before she could add anything there was a knock on the front door. Brickey, motioning to his wife to stay in the kitchen, walked through the living-room to a window beside the door. He pulled the curtain aside and looked out.

Speak of the devil, he said to himself. Aloud, he told those in the kitchen who was calling. 'It's the banker and your friend Voles, Nate.'

'No friend of mine,' Nate said, rising from the table and moving so as to be between the women and the new arrivals as they followed the sheriff back into the room.

'Good evening, Mrs Brickey, Mrs Harmon,' Runkle said, his voice smooth and friendly. 'I saw this young man coming down here and thought it would be a good time to discuss a trip out to your ranch, Mrs Harmon.'

Voles had stepped aside and stood next to the open doorway, his back to the wall. Nate, looking at him, let a smile lift his lips as he noticed the dark bruise along side the big man's face. Voles, seeing the smile, tensed and started to move toward Nate, only to be stopped by his boss.

'Now, boys, let's not have any of that. You have a job to do, Dutch, so relax.' The big man stood still for a moment, then with a scowl at the relaxed-appearing Nate, backed to his place against the wall.

'Nate,' Sheriff Brickey said, 'I didn't have a chance to ask you, but would you take my place tomorrow and ride out with Voles to Sarah's place? I guess we'd better take a look for the missing jewelry before the judge gets here.'

Nate's smile didn't grow much, but he felt it bubble up inside. All of a sudden he was sure who the unknown rider at the Harmon ranch house had been. With a quick glance at Sarah, Nate realized that this settled the question of her innocence.

'Now, Sheriff.' Nate shook off the giddy feeling to hear the banker say, 'That shouldn't be necessary. You sent Dutch out to escort Mrs Harmon in originally, surely you can put your trust in him again.'

'Maybe. But Mrs Harmon has asked for Nate to go along. It is her place, after all.'

'Yes. Well, possibly it would be better if the two men were there, as witnesses to what they find,' Runkle said, his eyes darting to the big man still standing against the wall. Voles didn't see the look, he was busy, Nate noticed, staring at Sarah.

'Or not find.' Nate smiled. 'Leave early, Voles? First light?' He added, turning to the bigger man, 'From what I'm told it's a good day's ride, round trip.'

'What? Oh, yeah. Sure, first light.'

'Well, then,' Runkle said, smiling his best trust-building smile again and placing his hat firmly on his head, 'that's settled. We'll be on our way. Come along, Dutch.' He nodded to the ladies, then led the way to the front door and out of the house.

'Dutch,' the banker said as the two men walked up the dirt street, 'Don't get starting any fights with that young man. Not until you find the jewelry and deliver it back here. I want both of you delivering it to the sheriff.'

'Aw hell, I could shoot him and bury his body in the pucker-brush and nobody'd ever find him.'

'No!' Runkle said, grabbing the bigger man by the arm. 'Listen to me. You bring the

115

jewels back. Both of you. That'll clinch the deal. Old Brickey'll have to put the widow Harmon in jail and I'll be able to make my offer. With her conviction a certainty, she'll be more willing to make a deal. She signs the ranch over to me and leaves the territory. And you take over as my ranch foreman. But you must do it just as I'm telling you. No fights and both of you come back together.'

'Yeah, yeah. I understand. But after we bring the jewels back, then I can take that busybody apart?'

'After the jewelry is in the hands of the sheriff, you can do what ever you want with him,' Runkle said, already thinking his own thoughts. 'C'mon, I'll buy you a drink.'

CHAPTER 15

Back at the Brickeys' kitchen, Nate was just finishing the piece of pie the sheriff's wife had cut for him. Why not tell the sheriff and Sarah about his finding the necklace and brooch? he asked himself.

'Something wrong with the pie?' Sarah asked, seeing his hesitation.

'Huh? Oh, no. I was just thinking. I wonder why Runkle wants to send us out to your ranch now?'

'Wal,' Sheriff Brickey said, looking at the last slice of pie left in the glass pie-plate. He pushed it toward the young man, but wasted no time when Nate shook his head and pushed it back. 'Wal,' he went on between bites, 'I guess his missis is putting a lot of pressure on him. She seems to set a lot of importance on the family heirlooms, you know. Women set a lot of store by things like that.'

'Roy, of course we do,' the sheriff's wife said, her voice soft and, Nate thought, a little sad. 'Don't you go making fun of us for it, either. We women don't have a lot to remind us of softer, gentler times out here in the territory. I can understand why poor Mrs Runkle fears for her mother's brooch and necklace.'

'My mother didn't leave me anything like jewelry,' Sarah said in the same kind of voice. 'Fact is, the ranch and all the hard work my father and mother put in to building it is all they left when they died. Guess that makes the ranch my family heirloom.'

Nate drank the last sip of coffee, placed his cup on the table and stood, retrieving his hat from where he had placed it on the floor

117

under his chair.

'Guess if I'm going to ride out early, I'd better find my bedroll. Mrs Brickey, and Sarah, thank you for the pie and coffee. Sheriff, I'll stop in and see you when Voles and I get back tomorrow.'

'I'll walk you out,' Sarah said with a glance at the Brickeys. Nate nodded and, turning to lead the way out of the kitchen, didn't see the older woman put her hand on her husband's arm, stopping him from following.

On the front porch, with the door closed behind them, Sarah faced Nate. 'I really meant what I said, Nate. I didn't steal anything from anybody. And my ranch is all I have. It's everything I'll ever have. Really, it's about all a person would need. Even the banker, Runkle, thinks so. He offered to buy it from me a number of times.'

'He did? Seems like he wants to own everything. I guess that's what bothers me. But don't worry, I know you didn't take old lady Runkle's jewels,' he said. Again the question came to him, why not tell her about finding the jewels. Could it be that he didn't want this to end too soon? He'd just have to get on his horse and ride south and maybe he wasn't ready for that yet.

'Nate,' she asked, breaking into his

thoughts. 'Why are you so adamant about going to California? It's none of my business, of course, but what's in California?'

'Oh, nothing really. Guess it's because I've never been there. Never been anywhere. I was born in a wagon coming over the trail and when we got to Oregon City my father started the feed-store. That's all I ever saw really, the farms and the people around there. There was a lot of produce and lumber sent by ship to California from around there and I always wanted to go see what that country really looks like. I heard people talking about it, but I want to see it myself.'

She watched his face as he spoke, but looked down at her hands before speaking.

'You should think about what happens after you don't find what you're looking for there. This is a good country and will be a good place to grow with. After this is over and the judge frees me, I'll need someone to help out at the ranch. I know this is forward of me, but there's room at the ranch for a foreman.'

'Well,' Nate said, flustered, 'I don't know. I would like to see California.' He had been nervously holding his hat by the brim and turning it over and over, but suddenly he jammed it on his head and went down the steps.

'I'd better go. Goodnight, Mrs Harmon. I gotta get up early. I'll talk to you tomorrow.' He knew he was talking too fast, but he couldn't help himself. 'Goodnight.'

He was almost running as he said the last and turned toward the center of town. He wasn't sure, but over the crunch of his boots in the dusty street, he thought he heard a soft chuckle come from the young woman still standing on the porch.

Nate was saddled and ready before Voles the next morning. After accepting a hot cup of coffee from the old man at the town corral, he settled back against the east wall, the wall facing the clean, bone-warming heat of the early morning sun.

'You recall my mentioning a man came looking for you a couple days ago?' Tex asked, sipping his coffee.

Nate carefully tested his coffee, nearly sacrificing a lip. How did it stay so damn hot so long? he asked himself And how can that old man drink it without burning his mouth?

'Reason I mention it is that fella was by last evening, again. Wanting to know about you but not wanting me to know that was what he wanted. A foolish man, I'd guess.'

'Who'd he say he was?' Nate got a small

sip at last, burning his tongue slightly.

'Didn't say, exactly, but it was the same man what was asking about you before. He didn't ask for you by name, though. No, he was asking about the owner of that pack-horse of yourn. That's what he asked about just about the time ya rode out of town, I guess. Yeah, it was the same day ya took that ride out to the Crooked River ranch.'

The same day Harney had tried to stop him on the trail, Nate thought, but didn't say anything, wondering what he was going to do about the man.

Tex sipped more coffee, obviously enjoying it. Nate still couldn't quite stand the hot liquid. He tossed the coffee out, carefully placed the cup on the step and mounted his horse. Not looking at the old man in the eye, he waved and went to find Voles.

CHAPTER 16

Until they were out of sight of anyone watching from town, the two men rode side by side. Once lost from view, without saying a word, Nate let his horse drop back a little, letting Voles get slightly ahead. Dutch didn't notice. He was busy planning how he'd take care of the smart-mouthed man riding with him. His time would come, and it would be worth the wait, the big man thought.

Runkle said not to do anything until they found the jewels and brought them back. All right, he could wait, but that didn't mean he couldn't plan. Gawd, he'd smash that smile off his stupid face. The thought brought a smile to the big man's own sunburned face.

Nate couldn't see the smile, but he noticed Voles sitting straighter in the saddle. Probably dreaming about kicking some orphan child or a stray dog, Nate said to himself.

Curly noticed the two riders first. 'Hey, Hank, we got company.' The three Harmon hands were at the breaking-corral next to the barn, topping off a dozen or so horses they had herded in from the big meadow.

'Hey, ain't that the fella that helped us the other day? What'd he say his name was? Gawd, I can see his face but I jest can't think of his name,' Curly said with a shake of his head.

'You been out in the sun too long, old man,' Hank said watching as the two men rode down into the ranch yard. 'Nate. His name is Nate. The other is that bastard Voles. Guess I'd better go see what they want. You two finish up here.'

'Sure. Lee, you see how it helps to be the big cheese?' The older man turned to the youngest of the three. In a mimicking voice he teased Hank, '"You boys finish up the work and I'll ride over and welcome the dudes to the ranch." Oh, yes, being foreman is certainly a good thing.'

Hank didn't respond, just opened the corral gate and rode through.

'Howdy,' he said, having ridden the short distance to the riders who had pulled up in front of the big house. Nodding to Voles, he started to say something to Nate when he caught the younger man's slight headshake. He decided not to go very far with his greetings.

Voles, as if it was his natural right, swung down from his horse without saying anything or being invited.

'We're here to search for evidence. Sent by the sheriff,' he said with almost official finality. He tied his horse to the porch railing and turned toward the steps.

'Wait just a damn minute,' Hank said, his right hand on the grip of his holstered pistol.

Nate, still sitting his saddle, spoke up. 'You

part of the Harmon crew? Mrs Harmon and the sheriff asked if we'd come out and look for some jewelry that is supposed to be missing. Evidence for the judge.'

Both Hank and Voles had turned to Nate as he spoke, but only the ranch hand seemed to notice that Nate was smiling.

'Wal,' Hank said, stepping down from his horse and leaving the reins dangling. 'Guess if the boss lady said, then it's all right.'

'Now how about this,' Nate said, swinging down. 'Why don't you just come along with us? Sorta make sure we don't just run off with the wrong jewels.'

Voles started to object, then decided that having more witnesses could only help Runkle's case. He nodded in agreement.

'Yeah. You just come along and keep an eye on things.' Once he was running this place the tall cowboy would be the first to go, he decided.

Nate looped his reins around the porch railing and followed the two men through the front door. He watched as Hank stopped in the center of the room and waited. This was the owner's house and he was slightly uncomfortable about walking right in.

Voles, Nate noticed, took a quick look around the room, stopping only briefly to look at a bookcase before moving on to the fireplace. Huge and made of water-smoothed rocks, a polished split-log mantel was covered with a variety of small glass knick-knacks. The kind of thing a woman would have around to make a house more of a home, but which a man would be afraid of breaking.

The big man quickly tired of playing around. Time to get down to business, he decided. After giving the things on the mantel a quick glance, he turned and headed for the bedroom door.

'Hey, do you have to go in there?' Hank asked, embarrassed, his right hand once more dropping to his holstered pistol. 'That's Miz Harmon's bedroom.'

'It'll take just a moment to check it out and see there's nothing there,' Nate said softly, following Voles closely into the room. 'Old Dutch is one quick searcher, can't you tell?'

Voles walked across the room, stopping suddenly when he didn't see the banker's jewelry on the dresser top. Turning to the ranch foreman, he demanded, 'Who's been in here?'

'Why, nobody that I know of. Not since Miz Harmon was here, before you took her into town. 'Course, we been out on the big

125

meadow a lot, but I ain't seen anybody fooling around until you came riding in.'

As Voles caught Nate's smile his scowl deepened. That smart punk knew something, he decided; he's just too happy for his own good.

'Well, Dutch,' Nate couldn't help asking, 'where you going to look next?'

'Damn you,' Voles said as he pushed past Hank and stomped out to his horse. He jerked the reins free, swung into the saddle and cruelly spurred his horse into a quick gallop back the way he had just come.

Nate and Hank stood in the yard and watched without saying anything. The foreman slowly rolled a cigarette.

'Don't worry about it,' Nate said. 'I think things are going to work out for your boss lady.'

'What the hell is going on?'

'Old Dutch really thought he'd find the evidence that'd prove Mrs Harmon is a thief. Now, well, we'll have to wait and see what happens. But don't worry, it'll work out.' He gathered up his reins climbed into the saddle. 'And thanks for not letting on we had met before.'

'That bastard's too sure of hisself. Didn't know what you was up to, but I could see you was riding him a little and that's good in my book.'

'I got to get back to town. I expect Mrs Harmon'll be back here in a day or so.'

'Hope so. She's a good person. Been hard on her, keeping things going after her husband got killed.'

'Killed? I thought it was an accident.'

'Don't think so. I rode up there, where he was supposed to have fallen. Just not likely. No tracks or anything. But it was an unlikely place for an accident. Hard to say, though, what really happened. It just didn't seem likely.'

'A lot of this doesn't sit right,' Nate said. 'Well, I'll do what I can to help her, then I'm off to California.'

'Oh? I sorta had the feeling you'd hang around. She could sure use the help here, you know. Foreman or something.'

'No, I'm on my way south. Thought you were her foreman?'

Shaking his head, Hank smiled. 'Not me, or any of us. Don't mind the work, but, hell, I ain't one to boss anyone or any ranch. We're just the hired hands.'

As he took up his reins Nate reached down to shake Hank's hand.

'Gotta ride. Thanks again for your help.'

CHAPTER 17

Voles was fuming. What the hell had happened to the necklace and brooch? He'd left it on the dresser in plain sight, now they were gone. That damn hired hand, Hank, had to be lying. He must have gone in and picked the stuff up himself, then said nobody had been around since the Harmon woman had been taken to town. He had to be lying.

'Wait a minute,' he said out loud, sawing back on the reins, pulling his horse to a stop. What did that lanky cowboy say? Something about not seeing anyone near the ranch house since Voles had come to take Miz Harmon back to town. Yeah, but that couldn't be. He had made sure all three hands were out in the far meadow when he'd gone to the ranch after the widow woman. Someone had to have told the foreman about it. Someone....

'Damn that loud-mouthed bastard!' The ears of Voles's mouse-colored horse lay back as he heard his rider's disgusted yell. Then before the beast could do anything but react, he was thrown into a hard run by jabs from both spurs.

It was late when Nate eventually rode back into town. Tired and covered with trail dust, all he could think about was seeing Sarah again. It would be good to see her face when she was told about the missing jewelry.

How could that make such a difference to him, though? He had only seen the girl for the first time a few days ago. In those same days someone had tried to hold him up, a big bully had picked a fight and he'd gotten involved with some stolen jewelry. But overriding it all was the woman now staying at the sheriff's house.

Sarah Harmon had been thinking about Nate Ragan, too.

'I know Nate and that Voles man won't find anything,' she said to Mrs Brickey. All day she had been up and down, first helping with the breakfast dishes and then, later, hanging blankets to air from long lines strung up outside between two trees. Now, in the afternoon, the women were back in the kitchen, enjoying a cup of tea.

'I mean, I hope they find Mr Runkle's jewelry but not at my house. Oh, you know what I mean.'

'Things are going to work out, dear. Don't

you worry. I think that nice young man will help you no matter what,' the older woman said.

'He has been so helpful.'

'And have you noticed the way he looks at you? I would almost guess he's sure giving his future a second thought.'

'No, he says he's heading for California. There's nothing to keep him here, anyhow.' But as she said the words, she remembered the way he had looked at her that first time. It had been a long time since a man had looked at her like that. Her husband had, for a while. But it was soon clear that Jess liked what he found at the Miners' saloon more than what he found at the ranch. Maybe it was a poker table, but Sarah wasn't sure.

The sheriff's wife frowned as she watched the other woman's face darken. Not sure whether she was worried about the theft charge or having Nate Ragan ride away, Mrs Brickey didn't say anything, just got up to refill the teapot with hot water.

Nate had already climbed wearily from the saddle and was tying the reins to the fence in front of the Brickey house when he stopped. Maybe it should be the sheriff he reported to. No, he decided, he'd tell Sarah first and then ride back to the sheriff's office. Using his hat, he tried to beat the dust from his clothes as he walked up the path to the porch. He knocked on the door and waited. Probably, he thought, he had better stay on the porch, no reason to pack all that dirt into the house.

But Mrs Brickey wouldn't hear of it. 'No, you come right in. The coffee's hot and Sarah can't wait to hear what you found out at the ranch. Neither can I. Go right through to the kitchen and sit down.'

'Ma'am,' he said tiredly, 'all day I've been sitting. I'll stand if you don't mind.' He stopped speaking as, walking into the kitchen, he found Sarah standing by a chair, looking searchingly into his eyes. It was only because she's worried about the jewelry, he thought, but having her look at him like that sure made him feel good.

'Hello, Mrs Harmon,' he said quietly, stopping and holding his hat-brim with both his hands.

'It's Sarah, remember?' she said with a smile.

'Well, seems like it's been Mrs Harmon all day, talking to your man, Hank, and all.'

'Here's your coffee,' Mrs Brickey said, smiling at the shyness of the young couple. 'Now tell us what you two men found at the ranch.'

'Nothing,' he said, his face breaking into a big smile. 'And you can bet that didn't make Voles very happy. He was fit to be tied, I guess.'

'I wonder where the necklace and brooch are?' Sarah asked, sitting down at the table. 'If I didn't take them, and Mrs Runkle doesn't have them, where could they be?'

'I wonder,' Mrs Brickey said, 'if maybe that Voles doesn't know more than he's letting on?'

'Well,' Nate said a little smugly, 'I don't want to say too much, but I think it'll all be over in a day or so.'

'What do you know that you're not telling us,' Sarah asked, her eyes never leaving his face.

'Nothing. But don't you worry. Now, thank you for the coffee, but I think I'd better go talk to the sheriff.' After giving Sarah another big smile, Nate left the house and headed back to town and the sheriff's office.

'Evening, Sheriff,' Nate said, closing the office door behind him.

'Well,' the lawman said, motioning Nate to a chair, 'I saw Voles come riding in. He didn't stop to share any news with me. Then

I watched you ride by, like a bee to a pretty flower, I said to myself. Figured you'd want to tell Miz Harmon 'fore you gave any thought to me. After all, I'm just the sheriff who asked you to take that ride in the first place.'

'Yeah, guess I should've stopped but I didn't want Sarah worrying more than she had to.'

'Didn't find anything out there, did you?' Nate shook his head. 'Didn't figure you did. Voles would've been the first one in the door, with Runkle right behind him yelling for me to bring Miz Harmon down here to a jail cell. Now I got to wonder, who did take those jewels? Maybe nobody. Maybe the banker was pulling a slick on the widow.'

'Maybe,' Nate said, thoughtfully.

'Now what the hell do you know that you're not talking about?'

'Nothing. That's the same question your wife asked me. I don't know anything,' Nate said, with a wide yawn. 'Guess I'll go get some supper and a good night's sleep. Probably be riding on, tomorrow.'

'And what about Miz Harmon?' the lawman asked. 'Say, if there's no proof she stole the banker's jewels, there's no reason to hold her, is there?'

'No, I wouldn't think so.'

'How about you seeing she gets home tomorrow? It's too late for her to ride home tonight.'

'Why? She knows the way to her ranch, doesn't she? Seems all I've done lately is ride back and forth to her place.'

'I don't know about that Voles. And I don't know about the jewels. I'd sure feel a lot better if you'd ride alongside her when she leaves town, that's all.'

'Aw, well,' Nate said, 'right now I'm so tired that the thought of riding anywhere makes me hurt. I'll talk to you tomorrow morning.'

'Not that it would be a hard job. Or one so odious, either. She sure is pretty, ain't she?'

'Yeah, she is that. But don't go planning anything. I'm riding for California, remember?'

'Uh-huh,' Sheriff Brickey said. 'I'll have her all ready to go after breakfast. Say ten o'clock, all right?'

'All right, but then I'm off, riding south.'

'Sure thing. Hear it's awful nice down there,' Sheriff Brickey said, smiling as he turned back into his office.

CHAPTER 18

'What?' Runkle couldn't believe what he had just been told.

'I said the jewelry weren't there. I don't know where it is,' Voles said, watching as the banker's face turned white.

'Tell me again,' Runkle said, turning away and pulling aside the heavy drape covering the window of his front room. 'You left them on a dresser in the Harmon woman's bedroom, but when you and that meddling Ragan went there today, they were gone? Who else could know about them?'

'Nobody. One of the hired hands said nobody had been out there. But he could've been lying, I guess.'

'You guess. Why would he lie?'

'Wal, he said nobody had been out to the ranch house since I took his boss lady and brung her to town. Nobody saw me do that. I made sure all the crew was over in the big meadow 'fore I went to get her. Someone told him that I was the one to cart the widow woman off and I think that was that bastard, Ragan.'

Runkle thought for a moment. As his anger faded away, he thought over all the comings and goings the stranger had been doing with since hitting town.

'He has been showing a lot of interest in the Harmon widow, and he did ride out there about the same time you hid the jewelry. Yes, he could have my wife's jewels.'

He turned away from the window and pointed a finger at the bigger man who stood, holding his hat in both hands, in the middle of the living-room. 'Find him and watch him. If you get him alone, beat the truth out of him.'

'What happens if I kill him?'

'You better not, damn you. At least not until we have the jewelry back. After that? Well, then I don't care.'

Neither man noticed someone behind a partly closed door, listening. Both men should have felt the bleak glare of hate on the face of Mrs Runkle, it was so strong. Quietly, she turned away, closing the door behind her.

Voles first checked to see whether Ragan's horses were still in the town corral. The gray pack-horse was there, but Ragan's riding-horse wasn't. The old man said he didn't know where Ragan was spending the night. Once this was over, Voles promised himself, he'd take a minute to wipe the smile off that old bastard's face.

Voles recalled having seen Ragan get a clean shirt out of a pack in the old trappers' cabin. Looking there, he saw the man's packs were still hanging from a rafter. All over town he searched until, shortly before midnight, after checking at the saloon a couple times, the restaurant and the hotel, Voles gave up. He'd have to wait until morning.

Probably, he figured, Ragan was sleeping at the sheriff's office, or even at the sheriff's house. Maybe with that damn Harmon widow. Remembering how she looked wearing the handcuffs, all beaten down, Voles swore.

'She'd've been mine, if that damn Ragan hadn't happened by.' And that would have been fine. She wouldn't be so high and mighty, once she learned exactly how her husband had died.

Well, he thought, she could still be his, after Ragan told him where the jewels were. After he took over her ranch, he'd have time for her.

CHAPTER 19

Nate had stopped by the general store and, seated in a chair tilted back on the boardwalk in front, he cut open a can of tomatoes and made a meal. Paring slivers off a block of rat cheese with his pocket-knife, he watched as Voles left the banker's big house and rode his horse down to the corral. After speaking to the old man there, Nate watched as the big man turned down toward the river and out of sight. Probably going to the trappers' cabin, Nate figured. Looking for him.

Well, maybe he'd ride out a ways to sleep tonight. He finished his supper, untied his horse and led him around back. Making sure his bedroll was tied on behind the cantle, Nate swung up and rode quietly toward the river. He stopped once to watch the searcher go back towards the business section, waited until it was clear, then rode down river a mile or so until he found a soft sandy place. He spread his bedroll, pulled blankets up to his chin and, using his boots for a pillow, closed his eyes.

Tomorrow, he told himself, things should be cleared up and he could head out, south to California.

Nate came awake slowly to the noise of a big black raven giving him hell from just a few feet away from his blanket-wrapped toes. Lying flat on his back, he ignored the clamoring bird and looked up through the branches of a huge pine-tree at the blue sky. Very nearly the same shade of blue as Sarah's eyes.

He sat up in his bed and chuckled as the squawking bird jumped away in fright, only to land on one of the boulders in the middle of the river. Above the sound of the rushing water, the young traveler could hear another rushing sound, that of the wind through the trees. What a peaceful place, he thought. A perfect place to bring Sarah for a picnic.

He shook his head, got up and put together a small fire. While water in his coffee-pot came to a boil, he washed in the river and rolled his bedroll. Once the water was hot, before dropping in a handful of crushed coffee beans he poured out enough water to shave with. Enough of that, he thought, no more thinking about picnics with Sarah or anyone else. Today he would head out. First he'd retrieve Mrs Runkle's jewels and return them. The widow Harmon could then go home and he'd ride south.

He couldn't tell exactly why he hadn't already returned the missing necklace and brooch, or at least given them to the sheriff. Something wasn't right and if he simply did that he'd never know what that was. But he was not staying here, so what did it matter to him? A couple days' riding and he'd be out of the high desert and back into the mountains. There would be plenty of peaceful camps like this one, once he was in the tall pines of the high mountains. Then he could take his time riding down into the Rogue River valley and on south to the gold-country.

A good thing he wasn't in a hurry. Why, once he was in the mountains he could take a few days to catch some trout and sleep late. Yeah, just as soon as he returned the jewelry.

CHAPTER 20

Voles hadn't given up the search for Ragan until very late. But nobody had seen him and the big man couldn't even find his horse. When the rest of the town quieted and even the saloon was closed, he had hunkered down behind a bush across the way from the sheriff's house. The only answer, he decided, was to wait.

After a while it came to him that if Ragan was in the dark house across the way, his horse would have to be close by. Quietly he circled around to the small stable and corral behind the house. Two horses stood hip-shot in the bare dirt of the enclosure. Neither was Ragan's.

'Damn,' he said quietly, thinking of the wasted hours he had spent behind that brush, waiting.

Once more he searched though the town's back streets ending up at the town corral. Nothing. At last he rolled himself in his blankets alongside the trappers' log cabin and slept.

After he'd sent Voles on his way, the evening before, Runkle had finished some banking paper work, blown out the lantern in his second-floor office, and gone home. He came into the house and quietly opened the bedroom door, hoping not to wake his wife.

He need not have worried. She was already in bed, lying wide wake, cloth curlers pinching her hair into tiny knots. She had things to think about, she couldn't sleep. Things were falling apart, she realized, having overheard her husband and that big, dirty man, Voles, talking. Her mother's cameo brooch and pearl necklace were really missing. John had sworn nothing would happen to them but now they were gone.

Lying in bed, propped up by pillows, she felt her anger fade. Where it had been a blaze of bright, hot fury, it was now a small hard knot of smoldering hate.

She stroked that hatred by thinking back to why she married John Runkle and her years with him. He was the first man to pay attention to her, but soon after the ceremony it became apparent that it was her father's money he was interested in, not her. She knew she wasn't pretty, or dainty or even very feminine. Her father reminded her of that fact often enough. Her mother had died when she was born and he never missed a chance to remind her of that either. She had killed her mother, he told her.

When the successful businessman, big John Runkle, came to town, he looked around and began to court the merchant's only daughter. Clara knew better, but she wanted to believe in this handsome man, so she did.

As time went on, though, as deals went

bad and they had to move on, from one town to another, she slowly came to recognize what her marriage was. But she didn't believe it had to be. When they arrived in this backwater place, she told her husband this had to be it. The end of failures. He agreed. With the last of her father's money he bought himself some respectability and that gave his wife a role to play, an important role in this frontier town.

The scheme to get the ranch on the Crooked River had gone too far when she had discovered it, and now, as a result of her husband's stupidity, her mother's jewels were gone. Lying wide awake in the feather bed, she decided what to do.

When John came into the bedroom, he found her in bed, propped up by thick feather pillows. Without saying a word, he took off his coat and hung it in the closet. He was just starting to unbutton his vest when she spoke.

'I don't want you in this room tonight.'

'What?' He stopped to look at her.

'You heard. I don't want you in my bed again, ever. From now on you can sleep on the couch in the living-room.'

'Now, Clara, that's no way to talk to your husband.'

'John, you've spent all my father's money. You've lost my mother's jewelry and you haven't been a husband to me for a long time. You get out of this room. Tomorrow, if that brooch and necklace are not in my hands I'm going to Oregon City. There I'll find a buyer for the bank and the other businesses. Then I will divorce you.'

'Clara, you can't do that.' His face had turned red as she quietly explained her plans. For a moment she thought he was going to attack her. As her words hit home, his face seemed to get bigger and redder.

Quickly she brought her hands from under the covers.

A little double-barreled derringer was almost lost amongst her chubby fingers. With a thumb she calmly cocked one of the hammers back and said without emotion, 'I can and I will.'

Slowly the banker backed away. 'Honey, we can make out. Your mother's jewels have got to be somewhere. Hell, Dutch must have them. He's stupid enough to try to double-cross me.' He couldn't take his eyes off the little pistol pointing steadily at him. Looking down the tiny, deadly black barrels was, he thought, like looking into the face of a very angry rattlesnake. 'I'll get them and then things will be all right again.'

'Go away, John.' Her voice was calm and steady, as steady as her weapon.

Without another word, her husband turned and left the room, slamming the door behind him. Clara, after bracing the back of a wooden chair under the doorknob, carefully let the hammer on her pistol drop. Making sure it was close to her hand she fell asleep, a relaxed, satisfied smile on her face.

CHAPTER 21

As he rode back into town early the next morning Nate took his time, enjoying the ride along the wild river. Compared to a river like the Columbia, the Deschutes was only a good-sized creek. For that matter, compared to the river he now rode along, the Crooked River wasn't much for size, either. But unlike the narrow, shallow Crooked River, this was a truly wild river.

Not wanting to reach town too early, Nate made a leisurely morning trip of it. This was the way he would spend the days, he decided, once he left this desert country and reached the tree-covered mountains.

His plan for the day was simple. First he'd return the brooch and necklace to Mrs Runkle and then he would explain to the sheriff why he'd kept them secret. Or try to. Nate wasn't sure why he hadn't turned them over to the lawman and had instead, hidden them, but he would think of something.

After that, with Sarah cleared of any crime and free to go, Nate figured he would shake off the dust of this area and head south to California. Yeah, it would be good to be riding again. Except he really didn't want to tell Sarah goodbye.

'Damn it, horse,' he said with a frown, 'we don't have time to think of her like that. We've got some traveling to do.' Gigging his horse into a trot, he rode on up the river toward the trappers' log cabin and the jewelry.

After having a late breakfast at the Miners' saloon, Voles stood hip-shot against the long bar, nursing a glass of cold beer. What the hell, somehow the jewels had disappeared. But who cared about them enough to take them from the widow's bedroom? Nobody would want them, except that fat wife of Runkle's, he decided. They weren't worth a great deal and would be hard to sell. I sure

146

wouldn't keep them around. 'Course, he thought, I'd never keep a woman like that around, either. The widow woman, now that was a different thing.

Damn. The jewels were gone and Runkle was mad. Without them the banker's plan would fall apart and Dutch Voles would never get to run the ranch. Why not forget all the cute stuff, anyhow? Harmon's widow could have an accident just like her husband, couldn't she? Voles motioned to the bartender for another beer.

What would happen, he thought, sipping the foamy brew. The jewelry wasn't found so the sheriff would have to let the widow go. Maybe somewhere along the ride back to the home ranch, she could just disappear. That'd fit what Runkle wanted. And be a lot simpler than all this work of making her look like a thief.

Once more, seeing himself at the ranch as foreman, the big man stood straight and with a jovial smile tossed off the rest of the beer. Hell, if I take care of the Harmon woman, I'll deserve more than just the job of foreman. Doing a thing like that might be worth half-ownership.

But it wouldn't be a good thing to be seen leaving town after the sheriff let the widow go. It would be remembered if he rode out after she was freed. No, he'd ride out now and wait. Voles waved to the bartender, dropped a few coins on the bar, and strolled out in his distinctive shoulder-swinging strut to untie his horse. His smile grew as he thought of the young woman. If she didn't ride out to the ranch today, she'd certainly ride out tomorrow. He could wait. It would be worth it.

CHAPTER 22

Amos Harney watched Voles ride out in the morning, then later saw the man he was after come riding up from the river. He hadn't seen Ragan since he'd let him get away out on the trail and here he was, just as big and without a worry in the world. He hadn't gone after the gold. Thinking about it, Harney hadn't thought he had. When he heard in the saloon that this stranger was paying court to the Harmon widow, the owner of the land near the gorge, he was sure. Why would any-one want to search for a saddle-bag of gold nuggets and dust when there was the whole of the rest of the gorge to have? Somewhere in that gorge was the lost gold-mine those wagon train people had stumbled across.

Yeah, the only thing to do was to follow Ragan for a while. Sooner or later he had to break away and head for the gorge. Anyone would, if they thought they could find the lost mine, wouldn't they? Sure.

Harney wasn't the only one watching as Voles rode out. Runkle, just leaving his house, also spotted his man just as he turned eastward down by the big corral. The banker had not had a good night, sleeping fitfully on the hard leather couch. With the first sign of the coming sunrise, he didn't spend any more time trying to find a comfortable position and got up. For a long time he sat at the kitchen table drinking cup after cup of coffee thinking about his problems.

At last, feeling haggard and dirty, he left the house. It was not his normal habit to wear the same suit two days running, and never the same shirt twice. Clara didn't like it, but he felt his image called for a fresh shirt even if it cost a little extra for the luxury. Walking down the street toward his office he saw Voles as the big man rode out of town. Runkle knew he would have to talk to Voles.

Maybe he did have the jewels. It didn't seem likely, but the banker couldn't think of any other answer. He would have to find out.

Thinking about it, Runkle decided that out on the trail might be a better place to have his talk. Nobody to listen or see what happened. Voles had been getting a little grabby, wanting more than the few dollars he had been getting. Making the promise to make him the foreman of the Crooked River ranch was easy, but the banker never expected to follow through with it. No, that job would go to someone who could handle it, not a stumblebum like Voles.

Runkle turned back to the house, went around back to his small barn and quickly saddled his horse. He cut across the main street and rode out through the sagebrush toward the trail Voles was taking.

After getting the package of jewelry from the log cabin Nate skirted the main part of town and rode up to the banker's house. He put the reins over the fence, opened a gate and walked up to the front door. It was a heavy-looking door, with a pane of etched glass in the center. He was surprised when, just before he reached it, the door swung open.

'Good morning,' the stocky woman,

dressed for the day in a housedress covered by a full apron, said. She had heard her husband leave and then had watched as he returned for his horse. She wondered where he was going and why he seemed so furtive as he rode toward Main Street.

She was just turning away from the window when she noticed the stranger riding up the street. It took a moment to remember him as the one who told the sheriff he had taken Voles's gun belt from him. A friend of the Harmon woman, she recalled her husband saying. Ragan was his name, she remembered. Surprised when the man pulled up in front of her house and tied his horse at the fence, she waited until he walked up the path, one hand in a pocket of her full apron. Before he could knock, she opened the door.

'Good morning, ma'am,' he said, taking off his hat and smiling. A good-looking man, she thought, the kind who had never looked at her, not with any warmth, anyhow.

'If you are looking for my husband, he just left,' she said.

'No, ma'am,' he said holding out a small bundle of cloth. 'I just wanted to give this to you.'

'What is it?' she said, almost suspiciously. When she didn't get an answer, she took the bundle and carefully opened it.

'Oh,' she gasped as the pearl necklace and yellowed cameo brooch lay in the palm of her meaty hand. 'Where did you get this?'

'It doesn't matter, I guess. But I would like you to withdraw the charges of theft you made against Mrs Harmon, now that you got your jewelry back.'

Looking up at the cowboy, the banker's wife smiled. With her mother's jewelry back, there was nothing to stop her now.

'Of course. I think it was a big mistake in the first place,' she said, almost tentatively, Nate thought. Looking up at him slightly sideways, he guessed she was testing the waters. Did he remember the demands she'd made to Sheriff Brickey? The taller man was careful not let his expression change.

'Will you be seeing her or the sheriff? Please tell them I'll be willing to forget the whole thing.'

Nate smiled. 'Good. There is one other thing, though. I understand your husband's bank has a note on the Crooked River Ranch for five hundred dollars. I was told her late husband signed it. I'd like to clear that up also.'

'I'll do better than that,' she said, opening the door wide and stepping aside. 'Please come in for a moment.'

She led the way into the living-room and went to a desk. She took a pen, dipped it into a bottle of ink and wrote a few lines on a piece of paper. She blew it dry, she read her words and then handed it to Nate.

'I don't know why Mrs Harmon's husband borrowed five hundred dollars from my husband, but I have to believe it was not totally ethical. He gambled, you know, and I think my husband arranged for him to lose and then loaned him the money to pay off the losses. I would like you to give this receipt for the loan marked paid in full to Mrs Harmon. You can think of it as a reward for returning my property.'

Looking at the piece of paper, Nate smiled. 'Thank you. This will make Sarah ... uh ... Mrs Harmon very happy.'

As she turned the young man toward the door Mrs Runkle once more thanked him. 'It's so good to get this jewelry back. It is all I have of my mother. Now, if you'll excuse me, I have things I must get done,' she said, closing the door behind him.

Clara Runkle returned to the living-room, sat down in the large leather chair and touched the brooch, remembering how it looked pinned to her mother's dress.

CHAPTER 23

Runkle was sure he hadn't been seen leaving town. And even if he had been, his early morning ride could never be connected with Voles.

Someone was watching, though. Tex was at that age when sleep past daybreak was sought but never found. When he was a cowboy, getting up with the sun was part of the job. Now that he didn't really have any reason to get up early, hell, not even before noon if he didn't want to, he came awake at the slightest sound. Even that of the sun coming up.

And every day, once he was awake, he was up. His joints would start aching if he tried to stay in his blankets after coming awake. Once he had fed whatever horses were left in the corral, a simple matter of forking enough of the sun-dried hay over the poles, he had little to do. Except enjoy his main hobby ... sitting in the sun and watching the town come to life.

Like almost everyone else, Runkle didn't give the old man a thought. As far as the banker was concerned, the corral-keeper was part of the corral. That was, if he ever gave the hostler any thought, which he didn't.

But Tex watched. First as Voles rode past heading out of town, never looking at anything but his horse's ears. Then, a short time later, as Runkle rode his horse quickly across the main street, disappearing between two buildings.

'Some doings going on,' the old man said, comfortable in his chair, tilted back against the side of the hay-shed. 'Sure doesn't mean good for someone, don'tya know?' he asked nobody in particular.

A little later he watched as Ragan rode up from the river and headed around toward the residential section. 'Ah, now I don't have to guess where he's going. Kinda early, but then he's young and probably in a hurry like most young folks.'

Runkle spotted Voles about three miles from town. The banker pulled his horse to a halt in the shade of a large juniper tree and took a minute to think things through. It was time he took control of the situation, he decided. And that meant thinking carefully of what he was going to do and say.

Voles had to have taken his wife's jewels. The man wasn't very bright but he must believe he could play his own game and never be caught out. It was so obvious to Runkle because it was exactly what he would do, if the situations were reversed. So, what would be the best move?

He pulled his pistol from the holster belted high on his hip under his long suit coat, and checked to make sure every cylinder was loaded, knowing that if he needed it he would never have time to get it out of the holster before Voles could draw and shoot. After checking the short-barreled gun, he slipped it under the belt at his belly. Now, let old Voles think I'm only scratching my chest or stomach and we'll see who has the upper hand. The heavy man chuckled.

Hearing the rider coming up behind him, Voles stopped and turned his horse around to watch as Runkle rode up. He smiled a little when he noticed the suit-wearing city man riding with both hands holding tightly to the saddle horn.

'What you doing out here?' he asked as his boss stopped a few feet away. Runkle didn't say anything, just removed his hat to wipe his head with a large handkerchief. Then he replaced his hat carefully and once more placed both hands on the saddle horn.

'Ask you the same thing. I believe you said you were going to find that Ragan fellow and get the jewelry back?'

'I am. He wasn't in town last night. I looked everywhere. Maybe he's got the stuff. But maybe not. My guess is that that ranch hand, I forget his name, he must have been poking around and found the jewelry on her dresser before we went back out there yesterday. So, I figured I'd ride out and ask him about it.'

'Now that doesn't make sense. Old Hank has been on the ranch for years, worked for old man Noble. No, he wouldn't go into the widow's house, and he certainly wouldn't paw through her personal belongings. That doesn't make sense at all.'

'Well, hell then. I don't know. That fool Ragan didn't spend the night anywhere I could find so I couldn't ask him. I didn't know where else to look.'

'I have been thinking about the jewels. Clara heard you and me talking. If I don't bring them home to her, she's going to leave me.'

'Damn it, don't blame me. Hell, ask me and I'd say you'd get the best of the deal, she was to ride out. You wouldn't have to sneak out to Sadie's, you could bring that black-haired girl right up to your big house.' He

157

laughed softly when his jibe caused Runkle's face to go white. 'Anyway, I told you, I put the jewels on the dresser at the widow's house like you said. I can't help it if that damn Ragan or somebody took 'em, can I?'

Runkle placed his right hand flat on his chest and slowly started scratching. His movements were soft, as if his woollen vest had caused an irritating rash.

'But there is one other thing that could make sense,' he said softly. 'Whether you really left them as you said or not, I figure you have my wife's jewels. It's the only thing that figures. A stupid move, I'd say, but then you aren't really too bright. Where would you expect to sell them? Well, that doesn't matter. The thing is, I must have them back.' His fingers continued to scratch lightly, only lower now. Bare inches from the pistol tucked out of sight under his pants top. 'I must have them to take to Clara.'

Voles had been sitting slouched in the saddle. As he heard the other man's words and the tone of them, he slowly straightened. 'Why you self-important fool. Listen to you, telling me your problem. Well, I'm telling you, I don't have your wife's precious doodads. I left them on the widow-woman's dresser like I said.'

158

'All right.' Runkle's voice was not soft and calm. His fingers, never stopping their scratching motion, moved smoothly to the pistol. 'I'll get them myself.'

Voles frowned at the abrupt change. Anger still ruled him, but he wondered exactly what the businessman meant. He was still frowning when Runkle shot him.

The shot struck only slightly off center, hitting Voles in the middle of his chest. The small slug cut through his heart and tore a much larger hole in his back as it made its way out into the clean desert air.

Runkle watched calmly, his pistol aimed, ready to fire again if necessary. Voles, his upper body thrown sharply back, fell back over his horse's hip. The horse was used to gunfire and didn't move until its rider fell backward out of the saddle. That he was not used to and he quickly stepped away, stopping a few yards off to chomp a patch of dry cheatgrass.

Runkle quickly looked around, but didn't really expect to see anyone. He climbed out of his saddle and continued to hold his gun on the fallen man. Slowly and carefully he reached out and touched Voles's outstretched arm. No pulse, and already the slain man's skin felt cooler and slightly clammy. Voles was dead.

Going through the man's pockets took only a minute. Nothing. Maybe in a saddle-bag. Voles's horse shied away as Runkle walked up to him, probably nervous of the faint odor of blood or maybe because Runkle smelled different from his usual rider. A soft word and the horse settled down enough for the man to grab the hanging reins. There was nothing tied to the saddle. No saddle-bag or bedroll. Running his hands over the leather saddle, he found nothing out of the ordinary. He had nothing to take back to his wife.

Runkle went through Voles's pockets again. Still nothing. He stood over the body and thought out his next move. He'd just have to face his wife empty-handed. But before that there was the matter of Voles's body.

CHAPTER 24

It seemed to take the cook at the restaurant twice as long as it should have to fix Nate's breakfast as usual. The young man almost yelled that he was in a hurry, but then realized that he really wasn't. Relax, he told himself with a small smile. Brickey said she'd be ready after breakfast, about ten o'clock. Yelling at the cook wouldn't hurry things up. Anyway, once he was finished with this ride, he'd be heading south. At a very leisurely pace, so what was the point in hurrying now?

At last, breakfast over, Nate spent a few minutes checking the saddle's girth. It was unnecessary, of course. The saddle was still secure. But the activity did kill a few minutes.

Why am I wasting time? he asked himself, looking around self-consciously to see if anyone was watching. 'Cause I'm about to spend the next three or four hours riding with that blue-eyed beauty, the widow Harmon.

Shaking his head at the direction his thoughts were taking, he climbed into the saddle. Taking that ride to California was getting to be a lot harder than it was supposed to be.

As he turned his horse toward the sheriff's office he saw the man climb down from a buckboard. 'Morning, Sheriff,' he said, riding up. 'That the rig you're using to get around in, now?'

'Wal, I could use one of these if I had to, I suppose. Good thing my work is in town, though. No, this is for you and Miz Harmon.'

'Oh,' Nate said with a slight frown. 'I just

161

thought we'd ride out on horseback.' Somehow the trip in a buckboard was different from one on two horses, side by side.

'She's taking back some blankets and things, women things, clothes and such my wife gave her. You can leave your horse in the corral and pick it up when you bring the wagon back this afternoon.'

'Yeah, I guess so. Well, where is my passenger, anyhow?'

'Up to the house. You go on up and I'll take your horse down to the corral.'

Sarah was waiting and it only took a few minutes to load the small wagon. A thick, many-folded woollen blanket was placed on the hard, wooden bench, something that would be greatly appreciated by the time they reached the ranch, Nate knew.

'Look, Nate, Mrs Brickey packed us a lunch. We can stop along the way and have a picnic.'

'Uh-huh,' Nate answered a little uncomfortably. Mrs Brickey, standing in the yard waiting to wave goodbye, laughed softly.

'Now Sarah, you don't forget to stop in for a visit, the next time you're in town. I really enjoyed your stay.'

'Thank you. I don't know what I would've done if you hadn't invited me. Don't forget to tell the sheriff thank you for me.'

'You already told him, but I'll tell him again.'

Nate took up the lines to the pair of horses and gave them a light snap, gigging them into motion. 'Goodbye, Mr Ragan. Stop by when you get back to town. I'll have the coffee on,' the sheriff's wife said. 'You can tell me all about your ride.' Again, laughing softly, she gave a last wave and turned back to the house.

Harney watched as the couple rode past in the wagon.

'Boy, now that's something,' a pot-bellied storekeeper standing beside him said, shaking his head. 'That youngster rides into town and not only gets next to the best-looking widow woman in the state but is smart enough to know how good he could have it.'

Harney smiled and nodded in agreement. 'Yeah. That ranch must be worth a lot, being so close to the gorge, and all.'

'You betcha. Year-round water? Why, old man Noble claimed near a thousand acres, I heard. With that water source in his back pocket it'll be no time until he's the biggest cattle spread around.'

'Yeah, I guess.' Harney let a frown play

across his weather-beaten face. "Course, there's the gold to consider.'

'Oh, you heard about that, did you? Well, I reckon young Ragan is smart enough to know that the stories about gold can't be counted on. Not like having a ranch like that, anyhow.'

Harney's frown deepened. 'You don't think he'll be going on after the gold?'

'Naw. I talked with old Tex down at the corral. He figured all along that the boy's idea of the gold went out the window once he met up with the widow woman.'

Not going after the gold? Harney was dumbfounded. He turned abruptly and stomped away, leaving the storekeeper muttering behind him. That damn fool had been playing with him. Teasing him about the gold. He wasn't even going to get the saddle-bag and now he wasn't planning on hunting for the lost mine. All this time he'd been making fun of Harney. Yes, and old Calhoun, too. He shouldn't have done it, Harney mumbled to himself as he tightened the cinches of his saddle. Not to him and certainly not to his partner. Obadiah wasn't the most sharing, but he was his partner. Yessir, that damn Ragan shouldn't've played with them like that.

CHAPTER 25

Conversation between Nate and Sarah was slow getting started, but before they had gone more than a few miles from town he found himself telling the pretty girl sitting next to him all about his childhood in Oregon City. Talking and laughing, they rode right by the place where only a few hours earlier Runkle had met up with Voles.

After making his second search, Runkle pulled Voles's body by the shoulders well off the trail. On finding a crease in the landscape just big enough to hide it, the banker dropped it, rolling it out of sight. He kicked a few rocks, some dirt and bushes over Voles, then looked around once more. Coyotes and other animals would do a good job of getting rid of any sign of the body, Runkle decided. Possibly no one would ever know what happened to the man. Certainly, Runkle thought, nobody would care. If anyone asked him about it, well, with a man like that who could know?

The horse was another matter. Well, Runkle thought, maybe not. He pulled off the saddle, removed the bridle and used the reins to whip across the animal's rump. Surprised, the horse gave a leap and took off running. Runkle picked up the gear and carried it back off the trail to near where the body was hidden. Something else for the animals and weather to destroy.

After kicking sand over the tracks made by dragging the body off, Runkle once more climbed on to his own horse and headed back toward town. About a mile out, he turned off the trail to come into town from behind the hotel. Taking that short cut, the banker missed running into Nate and the widow Harmon just as they rode past the town corral.

Runkle rode up to the hotel's corral and got stiffly down. The morning's ride had taken longer than he had been on horseback in a long time. He stripped the saddle off and turned his horse into the pen. He'd think of some reason for leaving his horse there later, if anyone asked.

As calmly as possible, he walked out of the alley alongside the hotel and crossed the street. Waving to one of the old men sitting in a chair, tilted back against the wall of the

166

general store, he walked on up to his house. Runkle knew he'd have to tell Clara sooner or later. Might as well get it out of the way.

Without thinking, he made sure his pistol was free in the belted holster before climbing the steps onto the porch and opening the front door. He expected to find his wife in the kitchen and was surprised to see her sitting quietly in a leather chair in the living-room.

She hadn't pulled the heavy drapes open yet, and the room was in cool shadows. What sunlight leaked around the drapes gave the room a soft, rosy glow. He almost didn't see her sitting there, motionless.

'Hello, Clara. Why are you sitting in the dark? Let's open the drapes and let in some light,' he said with as big a smile as he could muster. He took a step toward the front windows, but halted abruptly when she said, 'No!' in a cold, hard voice.

He turned and faced her squarely. He had never seen her like this: sitting in the chair, hands in her lap, not moving. No real expression on her face that he could see in the half-light. Just sitting there looking at him.

'Where is my mother's jewelry?' she asked, her voice now so soft he almost leaned forward to hear.

'Now, Clara, I have to tell you the truth. I

just don't know. I thought Voles had taken them but he didn't. I don't know where it got to or who has it.'

As he talked he heard his voice rising in pitch, not getting louder but faster, almost rambling in his panic. He tried to slow down. Relax, he thought, get a hold of yourself. Don't let her get control of the situation. Just explain it so she'll understand.

'I followed Voles and we talked. I was sure he had them, but he didn't.'

'How do you know he didn't have them?' she asked, her voice still calm and quiet.

'Why, huh, I searched him. His pockets, his saddle, everything.' Get control, don't say too much.

'Did he let you do that?'

'Well, huh, no. I mean, he didn't want me to. No.' He could feel sweat breaking out under his coat and vest. Damn her. Moving slowly, he began unbuttoning his vest, his fingers slowly working from top to bottom towards his belt.

'Clara, I'm sorry. It was a chance to take over the Crooked River ranch, legally, and I had to take it. Something went wrong, but I'll make it up to you.' His left hand was under the bottom button of his vest and his right had moved back toward his pistol. He actually had his hand on the gun when his eyes saw the pearl necklace his wife was wearing. Pearls.

All movement stopped.

'Clara,' he said and as her hands moved he saw the brooch pinned to the lapel of her dress. 'Clara, what the hell is going on?' His eyes were glued to the off-white ivory cameo-brooch, his mind trying to figure what it meant. He didn't see the derringer until it was pointed at him and she pulled the trigger.

The heavy man didn't hear the sound of the gun going off, he only felt his head being struck before blackness closed out everything. The bullet struck him under the chin and blew out the back of his head, throwing his flat-crowned hat behind where he landed on the floor, one arm outstretched, the hand holding his pistol. Clara Runkle blinked, but didn't move. The noise had been a lot louder than she had expected.

CHAPTER 26

Sheriff Brickey was down the street from the residential section when he heard the single gunshot. He stopped, one hand on a hitching-post, frozen as he waited for a second shot or something to tell him what had happened. Nothing came.

Clara had not moved out of the big leather chair when the sheriff found her a few minutes later. She sat as calmly as she had all morning while waiting for her husband. The waiting was now over.

'I shot my husband,' she said quietly, tiredly. Brickey, looking down at the bloody mess, nodded.

'Why?'

'My mother's jewels,' she said touching the brooch. 'He killed Voles because he thought Voles had them. But I did.'

The lawman looked closely at her in the morning darkness. 'He did what?'

'He killed Voles this morning. He told me.'

'Well, don't that take all. Will you be all

right? I'll get someone to move the ... huh ... Mr Runkle.' Seeing the banker's pistol, he nodded. 'Guess the way it looks, you shot him in self-defense. I know he was worried about the jewelry.'

'That was the problem,' the woman said, still not moving. 'He wanted to blame the Harmon woman. He thought if she believed she'd get sentenced to jail he could get her to sign over her ranch in exchange for him dropping the charges. Voles had planted the jewels at the ranch, but when you sent him and Ragan out, somehow, they had disappeared. John followed Voles out of town this morning to accuse Voles of stealing them.'

'Well, I never believed Miz Harmon had taken anything,' the sheriff said, wondering whether he should mention the demands the woman had made a few days earlier. No, she would just claim she didn't know anything about her husband's plans at that time.

'I think he may have had something to do with the death of Mrs Harmon's husband, too,' the woman went on, still speaking softly and never taking her eyes off the man she had just shot.

'I don't know for sure,' she continued, her voice low but steady, 'but I overheard my husband and Voles talking last night. I couldn't hear everything, except the mention of Jess Harmon and then they both laughed.'

'Well, if Voles is dead, that's something we'll probably never know about. I'll get someone to help you,' Brickey said, moving toward the door. 'You better go lie down and I'll send someone over.'

Now where are the good women of the town when I need them? he asked himself. Finding someone to sit with the banker's wife turned out to be easy. Everyone wanted to know what had happened and a number of women were willing to come and help out. The town's undertaker removed the body, and Sheriff Brickey, knowing that Tex would know who did what and went where, walked down to the corral to talk with him.

'Yep, that damn bully, Voles, rode out of town early. Runkle, may he rest in more peace than he gave folks around here, he snuck out of town directly after. Cutting through the alley by the hotel, but he had to be following his man.'

'Maybe I ought to ride out along the trail to see what I can find out,' the sheriff said, not really looking forward to the pain such a ride would cause his leg.

'Wal, yeah, maybe so. Don't forget, Miz Harmon and Ragan rode out a bit ago, too.'

'Oh, hell. I plumb forgot about them. This all has something to do with Miz Runkle's mother's jewels. Maybe Runkle ran into them, too. You still got that old buckboard out back?'

'You already borrowed that. 'Bout the only thing I got is that old buckboard belonged to the Runkles when they rode into town. It's been sitting back there for a long time. Wheels haven't been packed or anything in years. Guess it'd work, but–'

'Never mind. Get it hitched up. Ragan and Miz Harmon may need help and it'd be all my fault for listening to that damn Runkle.'

Tex, belatedly getting the feeling of hurry the sheriff was experiencing, dropped a loop over the head of one, then another of the horses in the corral. The pair were soon harnessed to the weather-beaten buckboard.

When Tex followed the sheriff on to the hard wooden bench of the wagon, Brickey didn't argue. While both men were trying to find a comfortable spot to sit on, the hostler snapped the reins. For a few minutes the squealing from dry hubs made talking nearly impossible. The sheriff didn't try to yell above the noise, he simply pointed toward the east trail and then hung on as the small wagon lunged away.

As the dried grease warmed and spread over the packing in the hubs, the noise lessened, and Brickey could hear the old man talking to himself.

'I shoulda known, when I saw that damn Voles ride out, then Runkle, there would be trouble. Should've said something to Ragan and the widow, too. But they looked pretty good, riding along. And he thinks he wants to ride on to California. Hah! What a fool.'

CHAPTER 27

After taking his shot, Harney knew he would be expected to head north toward Powell's Store, not south into the desert. If anyone was interested, that is. Harney doubted anyone would be.

But if he rode south a couple miles, his trail would be lost in the sand. He could bear westward and come back onto the trail a few miles on down. Crossing from there he could then head north, passing Powell's Store and heading back to Shaniko. While he waited for the shooting to be forgotten, he'd hunt for the saddle-bag that Obie had hidden. It couldn't be that hard to find.

After deciding that Ragan had to be dealt with, he'd ridden out, keeping out of sight of everyone, and had followed the couple in their buckboard. After passing them he rode on until he found the perfect place for the ambush. It was just right, with a place to tie his horse, a small sand-bottomed ravine that seemed to snake away southward into the desert. Just the way he wanted to go.

As he shook his canteen he decided it was a good thing his plans were to spend only a few hours out here. If Ragan didn't come by, he'd fill it up when he got back into town. And if he got his shot, he could fill it at one of the ranches along the way. Either way, even with a half-empty canteen, he was all right.

Harney had watched the buckboard come in view. As they got closer, he saw that one was the widow woman and sitting closer to his side of the road was his target, Ragan. Harney smiled; it would soon be over.

From his position behind a large clump of sagebrush he watched as the wagon came slowly closer, the team just plodding along. Watching and waiting, he planned what he would do. When the wagon got broadside of his position, he'd shoot. Heading downhill, the wagon would go another good piece before it could be stopped. That would give him time to get away. No, if he missed or the bullet went through Ragan, it might hit the woman. That wouldn't be good. You just didn't harm a woman, not even accidentally. They'd never stop looking for him if that happened. He'd better shoot a little early, before it got even with him.

Harney watched as the wagon got closer. He could feel the sweat run down his back. The sun was almost directly overhead and hot. He had taken his suit-coat off sometime ago had folded it carefully and placed it over a large rock. But that hadn't helped much. Next time he had to do this kind of thing, he smiled at the joke, he'd be sure to find a shady place to wait.

But there would be no next time. Carefully, the perspiring man took aim at the man on the wagon seat. Slowly, his sights centered on the face of his enemy, his finger tightened on the trigger.

He wasn't expecting the rifle to fire, when with a loud crack he had shot the man. He watched in amazement and saw the woman's head fall to the man's chest. Harney watched and saw Ragan's arm fall, obviously comforting her as the team bolted, taking the wagon out of sight down the trail.

Turning blindly, he dropped the rifle and ran for his horse. He had shot the woman! In panic, leaving gun and suit-coat behind, he kicked the horse into motion. Away, he had to get away.

CHAPTER 28

While Nate and Sarah talked, neither paid any attention to the horses. They, not feeling any pressure from the reins, found a comfort in just walking along, following the well-worn trail.

Nate told Sarah all about his childhood, she told him about hers. She described her father and mother and her life on the ranch growing up, and he told her of life in Oregon City. He started to tell her of his plans for riding to California, but changed his mind. She pretended not to notice. Neither paid any attention to anything but each other.

Nate laid his left arm on the back of the buckboard's bench seat. Both his feet were up on the splashboard, the reins held loosely in his right hand, his whole body very relaxed.

He didn't hear the shot. The bullet hit him a glancing blow, striking him along the backside of his head, twisting it to the right, away from the girl. Relaxed as he was, his feet braced against the splashboard, his left arm instinctively fell across Sarah's shoulders, pushing her head down against his chest.

Sarah, hearing the gunshot, and feeling Nate's body jerk and go limp, ducked her head down. Almost without thinking about it, she grabbed the reins and snapped them against the horses' backs. The team, surprised, took off at a gallop.

Tex was the one who spotted the brushed-out tracks that let to Voles. He and the sheriff had been riding slowly, each watching for anything out of the ordinary. Following the half-hidden trail, they easily found where the soil had been recently disturbed. They quickly cleaned off the dirt, rocks and brush and were now standing over the shallow grave, considering how to get the body into the back of the wagon. That question was forgotten when they heard the far-off sound of a rifle shot.

Without a word, both men hurried back and climbed into the buckboard. With a snap of the reins, Tex quickly had them on their way.

'Someone mad at a coyote, maybe?' the older man asked the sheriff, without taking his eyes off the trail ahead. He wanted to miss the larger of the rocks, a broken wheel would wreck everything at the speed they were going.

'Dunno,' the sheriff answered, hanging on with both hands. 'Usually nobody'd waste the lead. There was only one shot, and it sounded quite a ways away, don't you think?'

'Yep, nothing this way 'cept the widow's ranch, and that's another five or six miles, I'd say.'

'Yeah, but don't forget, Miz Harmon and Ragan are somewhere ahead of us.'

'Damn! It'd be about right. Someone is shooting at 'em. Yee-hah, git on there,' Tex yelled.

The horses were slowing down from their run when the men saw the widow's buckboard. Sarah had stopped the team and had Nate lying down flat on the seat. She was holding a cloth against his head, trying to stop the bleeding. His chest was rising, slowly and steadily and the bleeding had slowed, with only a slight seepage filling the cloth.

Careful not to move the compress, she stood to look around. If the ambusher came

179

to check his shot, she wanted to be ready. She had taken Nate's pistol from his holster and had it in one hand. Seeing nothing, she searched for more cloth, something to bind Nate's head with. From his hip-pocket she found a handkerchief, really just a large square of unhemmed cloth. When she had tied it around his head she was able to put more pressure against the wound. His eyes were still closed.

The bullet, from what she could tell, had struck a glancing blow, leaving a furrow along the side of his head. She had almost fainted when looking at the wound, she had seen the white of his skull in the groove through his hair and skin. But he was alive. His face was white, with a single spot of red on each cheek, looking like face paint. He was injured, but still breathing.

Hearing the sheriff's wagon racing toward her, she stood and held the pistol ready. Her face was regaining a little of its normal color as she watched the wagon come to a halt and the two men climb stiffly down.

'Sheriff,' she said with worry in her voice, 'someone shot Nate. He's still alive, but he's hurt bad.'

'Let's take a look at him,' the sheriff said. Gently he pulled back one of Nate's eyelids and nodded. He placed a hand gently on Nate's chest, and saw that the young man's color was slowly returning.

'His breathing is all right and his face is getting back its color. We'll just have to wait,' he said, turning to look at the woman. 'Are you all right?'

'Yes, whoever did it was in those rocks, over that way,' she said, pointing toward a small knoll covered with clumps of sagebrush.

Tex left the group and walked to the area she had pointed out. Circling around, Tex came up behind the small rock and sage-brush-covered hill. He first found where a horse had stood. From the droppings, he figured the animal had probably been tied to a branch of a juniper tree for at least an hour or two.

He climbed to the top of the rise, from where he'd a good view of the trail. On top of a large boulder, the old man found the folded woollen suit-coat. Down below a little, he found a rifle half-covered in the soft sand. It didn't take an Indian tracker to see where the shooter had crouched to take his shot. A scattering of dead grass and twigs showed where he had jumped up and run for the horse.

Tex followed the running horse on foot for a short distance, long enough to see the direction and where the trail disappeared into the distance, southward. Taking the rifle and suit-coat, he walked back to the wagons.

'He's gone. Rode off in a hurry, didn't even take time to pick up his fancy coat or his gun. From the sign, I'd say he was in a panic. Probably scared him. Killing a man does funny things to a man, I've heard.'

Sheriff Brickey and Sarah had moved Nate back into the buckboard's bed. The wounded man lay quietly on a pad of blankets, his head cushioned by more blankets. His eyes were still closed.

'Any idea who the shooter was?' the sheriff asked.

'Wal, I think, maybe. This here coat looks a lot like that fella that's been in town asking a lot of questions about this young man, here. Can't recall his name, but Nate seemed to know who he was.'

Nate's breathing changed slightly, and a soft moan escaped from his lips.

'Wal, what do ya suggest we do with the boy, Sheriff,' Tex asked.

'Probably take him back to town. We go slow and he'll be all right, I guess. Surely can't leave him here.' Looking up at the old man, Brickey thought he saw something flicker behind the tired old eyes.

'Wal, yeah. I guess,' the hostler said slowly, as if in deep thought. ''Course, it's a lot closer to your ranch, ain't it, Miz Harmon?' he asked innocently.

'Yes,' she answered slowly, never taking her eyes off Nate's relaxed face. 'It's only a couple miles to the turn-off and then down to the ranch. Say five miles. If I drive slow, we could be there by late afternoon.'

'Now the way I see it, Sheriff, the shooter is riding off to the south. If Miz Harmon took the boy to her place, you'n me can ride out a ways and see where he goes. Probably be thinking about circling around, back to town. And we got to pick up Voles, too.'

Sarah looked up at the sheriff. 'I think that would be best,' she said. 'I can take care of him as well as anyone in town. I'll get the men to help me carry him inside. He'll get lots of rest and I can take care of him.'

The old man nodded in agreement and, unseen by the girl, nudged the sheriff. Brickey frowned, but after a moment's thought, agreed.

'I suppose you're right. Only thing we could do is take him to town and then have to find someone to care for him. And I'd like to catch up with the fella that owns that suit-coat.'

CHAPTER 29

Panic drove Harney, pushing him on. But eventually, many minutes after he'd pulled the trigger, his horse could go no farther. Winded, the animal stood, legs trembling, his big chest heaving, white foam covering his withers.

Harney stood high in the stirrups and looked back. Nothing. He climbed down stiffly, and hung his head as if as out of breath as his mount. Slowly, as the horse gained its second wind, the man also calmed down. He had shot the woman. It was a mistake. He hadn't meant to, but would anyone believe him? They'd hang him before he had a chance to convince anyone. And what could he tell them? That he was trying to kill Ragan?

He had to think. If they caught him, he was dead. There had to be a way out of this nightmare. He would have to leave the area, that was sure. If he were to live he would have to change his name, too. Take on an entirely new life, somewhere else. As he glanced back over his shoulder, it came to him. California. Nobody would know him in San Francisco or Sacramento.

He untied the canteen from the saddle and took a small swallow. Close to empty, he judged. Carefully he retied it to a saddle strap. As he looked around, though, his heart sank. In every direction all he could see was the same low, rolling hills of brown sand.

The horse had stopped on top of one of the low rises. Looking down, he could see that the breeze was beginning to blow the fine sand that seemed to cover everything. He watched as sand began drifting up against one side of low-lying bushes and clumps of grass.

Harney turned to look at the tracks left by his horse. They were filling in. The hoof-marks were the only indication of the way he had come and they were disappearing as he watched. He grabbed the reins and started walking in that direction, reins in hand, pulling the animal.

Harney took only two or three steps when he was brought up short. The horse wasn't following him.

He turned to yell at the beast, then watched in shock as the big animal's legs slowly folded. Silently, with only the sound of slithering, moving sand, Harney watched as his horse lay down, his big eyes huge pools of white pain. For the first time the man saw the blood-tinged foam that covered the animal's nostrils. When the eyes lost their sheen and glazed lifelessly over, the rider knew he was in trouble.

Panicking again, Harney started to tug at the reins. 'Get up, damn you,' he yelled. He rushed to the animal and yelled once again. He began kicking at the horse's neck. Off balance, he fell, landing flat on his back, sliding downward in the loose sand.

Stop it, you fool, he said, lying still where he stopped. You haven't time to panic. He sat up and felt the breeze a little stronger against his back. He had to move before all traces of the trail disappeared.

Harney took the canteen from the saddle, and gave the animal one more half-hearted kick, and started out, hoping he was walking in the right direction.

Sheriff Brickey and Tex rode their buckboard out away from the main trail, following the trail left by the fleeing rider. They followed as far as they could until, noticing the soft wind blowing against his face, the sheriff pulled up.

'Still headed south. And not letting up, it looks like,' he said, resting his forearms on his knees.

Tex, sniffing the air and turning his head slowly from side to side, nodded. 'Yeah, don't look as if he's makin' any turns. Heading due south. Smells like a storm coming up. Any wind coming, he's in trouble.'

He waited a moment to spit a brown stream over the side, then continued: 'Doubt if he'll show up back in town. Probably kill his horse 'fore long, the way he's running him, poor fool. Riding him like he's been doing there ain't no way he could carry enough water to keep that dumb beast going.'

Brickey nodded in agreement. Slowly he took up the reins and turned the team back toward the trail and town.

For a while neither man spoke, both thinking about all that had happened. 'Guess the widow will take good care of Ragan,' the sheriff said, not as a question but simply making a statement.

'Wal, I guess so. He talked a lot 'bout goin' to California, but, wal, we'll see.'

CHAPTER 30

Nate woke up slowly. His head hurt as though it was trying to burst from the pain. He opened his eyes, but quickly closed them tightly against the glare of sunlight streaming through a curtained window. Later, after falling back into a black, pain-free sleep, he once again came awake. This time the pain was a dull throbbing, as if someone was hammering on his skull with a hunk of wood. Without opening his eyes he moved a hand to his head. Carefully he felt the softness of a cloth band around his head. A lumpy mass on one side was the spot the fellow was hitting on.

The glare that had hurt his eyes before was now the soft light of dusk. Without moving his head much, he looked slowly around. Nate could see it was a quiet room. Walls that had been whitewashed long ago had a pleasant aged-yellow color in the evening's light. The room wasn't very big, not much more than space for the bed he was in and a chair and night table. A door was opposite from the curtained window and probably led into the rest of the house.

The question of whose house was answered as the door opened and Sarah Harmon stepped into the room, a kerosene-lantern held high. The soft light from the lantern gave her hair a warm look, almost like sun-softened honey. She was wearing a pair of men's pants, the waist cinched up tight by a wide leather belt. Her shirt, plain without frills was a soft faded-blue color. Lying down and unable to move his head much, Nate couldn't raise his head enough to see clearly but he relaxed, thinking of the last time he had seen her dressed like that. It had only been a few days, but it seemed like months since Voles had brought her handcuffed into that roadside tavern.

'Oh, good. You're awake. You had me scared for a while. I didn't think you'd ever wake up. How are you feeling? Are you all right?' Her voice rose in panic as he lay quietly watching her. 'Can you hear me?'

'Whoa – I'm all right, I guess. Just trying to figure how I got here. What happened?'

She set the lantern on the little table and reached over to feel his forehead. 'You were shot. The bullet put a big dent in the side of your head. Your hat probably helped. You had a fever for a while, but it's gone. I think you're going to be all right.' she said, smiling and sitting down in the chair.

'How long have I been here? I take it we're at your ranch?'

'Yes. I brought you here while the sheriff and the old man, Tex, went looking for the man who shot you. That was three, no, four days ago.'

As the evening turned to night and the world outside became dark, she told him of the shooting and the long, slow ride to the ranch. She was telling how Hank and Curly had carried him in and the care she had been giving him, when she noticed his eyes drooping. Within minutes, he was once more asleep. For a little while, she sat and watched him.

The next morning, the injured man woke up hungry. After attempting to get out of bed and falling back when his head began to throb, he decided to wait awhile. Soon, Sarah came in, bringing a breakfast of juice and soft-boiled eggs.

As he ate, she told him the sheriff had been out and told her the ambusher hadn't been found. Sheriff Brickey said he thought he knew who it was, though, from the suit-coat that had been found lying on a rock.

'The sheriff came out yesterday, before you

woke up. He rode his wagon out to see how you were getting along,' Sarah said. 'He said a cowboy, coming in from farther out, had ridden off the trail a ways to see what a bunch of vultures were after out in the dunes. He told the sheriff he found what was left of a saddled horse. The sheriff is thinking it belonged to the man that shot you.'

Nate lay still as Sarah brought him up to date, simply lying still, watching her face as she talked. After a minute or so, he said, 'I'd guess it was that fellow, Harney. He's the only one, other than the banker Runkle, wears a suit-coat all the time. Guess he gave up trying to get me to tell him about the gold.'

'What gold?'

Quickly he recounted being ambushed and finding Obadiah Calhoun and the pocket of gold the two men had apparently found in some gulch.

'Why, there has been talk about gold being found up in the gorge. There was a story that someone on a wagon train had found gold, but didn't mark it and could never find it again. Every so often some fool will go up in there trying to find it. Father was afraid someone would find it and change the river before it got through the gorge.'

For a minute Nate rested, thinking. 'Well,

if Calhoun and Harney did find something, it's lost now, what with both of them dead.'

'Sheriff Brickey said unless he was very lucky and was carrying lots of water he probably won't make it out of the dunes.'

Neither spoke for a few minutes. Nate liked looking at this woman.

'The sheriff brought your horses out, with your packs. Said to tell you that Mrs Runkle had left for Oregon City. She killed her husband, you know.'

'No, I didn't know that.'

'And Voles is dead, too. The banker shot him. I don't understand it all, and the sheriff didn't explain very much.'

Nate felt his eyes growing heavy. His gear was here, so he could ride on to California. As soon as he felt up to it, anyhow. No reason to rush. Wouldn't hurt to rest up for a while, he decided. He would answer Sarah's questions tomorrow. Yeah, there really wasn't any big hurry, he decided as sleep took over his thoughts.

Sarah watched as his face relaxed, a smile on his lips. Quietly she picked up the breakfast dishes and went out of the small bedroom. Looking back at the sleeping man, she smiled. Oh, it was good to have a man in the house again.